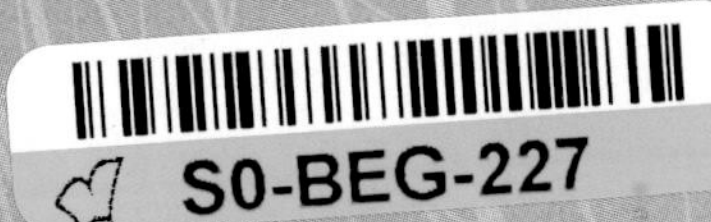


# VAMPIRE BOOK OF THE MONTH CLUB

RUSTY FISCHER

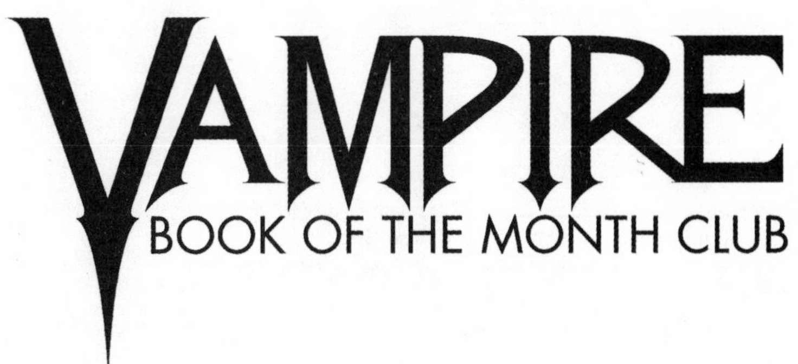


# RUSTY FISCHER

Medallion Press, Inc.
Printed in USA

Published 2016 by Medallion Press, Inc.,
4222 Meridian Pkwy, Suite 110, Aurora, IL 60504

The MEDALLION PRESS LOGO
is a registered trademark of Medallion Press, Inc.

Copyright © 2016 by Rusty Fischer
Cover design by James Tampa

All rights reserved. No part of this book may be reproduced or transmitted in any form or by any electronic or mechanical means, including photocopying, recording, or by any information storage and retrieval system, without written permission of the publisher, except where permitted by law.

Names, characters, places, and incidents are the products of the author's imagination or are used fictionally. Any resemblance to actual events, locales, or persons, living or dead, is entirely coincidental.

Cataloging-in-Publication Data is on file with the Library of Congress

Typeset in Adobe Garamond Pro
Printed in the United States of America
ISBN # 9781942546382

10 9 8 7 6 5 4 3 2 1
First Edition

WOODSON

# PROLOGUE

*Scarlet Stain takes a deep breath, kicks out the vent cover with her thick-soled boots, and before the heavy metal grate can clatter to the tile floor—thus alerting her captors—she reaches down to catch it with an expertly trained hand.*

*Years in the Afterlife Academy for the Exceptional Dark Arts have trained her well, and she quietly slides the grate to the side even as she pokes her long, slender legs through the small opening.*

*The drop is far, but she's been trained on much higher assaults, though it doesn't help that the floor is slippery. She lands silently, feeling a pinch in her left knee.*

*She looks at the old scar, resting there just between her long, knee-high boots and short, thigh-high black skirt: an old war wound, left by her archnemesis himself, the dreaded and powerful Count Victus.*

*She slaps her hands together, rubs them briskly as her martial arts instructor back at the Academy trained her to, and applies them to her wound. Once the healing warmth spreads through her knee, she stands, defenseless, looking around for something to use on her appointed mission. Fortunately, her escape route has dropped her right into the kitchen area.*

3 9222 03183 3978

*She grabs a paring knife and shoves it into the waistband of her short skirt, slips one more into the heel of her boot, and makes quick work of carving the tip of a spare rolling pin into a stake fit for Count Victus himself.*

*She stands, ready to do battle, and skulks to the kitchen door. Outside the greasy circular window a conclave rages, the annual meeting of vampire royalty. Fifty of the world's most powerful vampires are seated in one ultrasecret room deep underground.*

*This is the Council of Ancients, the best of the best, the most influential, wealthy, powerful, and lethal gathering of vampires ever held. And she is here to slaughter them.*

*All of them.*

*Every last stinking, bloodsucking, life-draining one of them!*

*That Scarlet was able to find the location of this year's conclave means little compared to the fact that she was captured so soon after arriving. The thought that it might have been a trap set by Count Victus has naturally entered her mind, but . . . what of it? She has a job to do, and—trap or no trap—the time is at hand. Now she has overpowered her captors, leaving them lying in pools of their own vampire blood, and has found the heart of the party in record time.*

*On the other side of the kitchen door, Count Victus sits at the head of a regal table filled with devastatingly handsome vampires. All are well over six hundred years old. All look striking enough to lounge around in tuxedos swilling scotch out of crystal glasses in some fancy cigarette ad.*

*But these men are lethal, and it is Scarlet's job to wipe them out, one by one. She knows it's a suicide mission to attack one such Ancient, but all fifty of them—in the same room—at one time?*

*Suicide: there's simply no other word for it.*

*She takes another deep breath, grabs her stake, and pushes through the kitchen doorway, odds be damned . . .*

I sigh, frown, and make some other woefully pitiful and decidedly self-indulgent author-type noises before closing the sleek silver laptop without saving the document.

Ugh, another one bites the dust!

Half an hour of work, a whole page of manuscript, flushed down the toilet. Or, in this case, that little bulging trash can in the lower right-hand corner of my laptop screen.

But it's the only thing to do.

It just doesn't . . . *feel* right, you know?

And it hasn't for some time.

I can already imagine the irate user comments on my latest book blog if the page I just deleted were ever to make it to print:

How did Scarlet find the conclave so easily? In book four you said Count Victus used his "cloaking scent" to mask his true presence. Have you forgotten so quickly, Nora?

How could Scarlet grab the air-conditioning vent before it clattered to the floor? Wouldn't a little thing we call "gravity" make that impossible, if not highly improbable? I mean, what's next? Are we going to find out her father is really Stretch Armstrong in book six?

Wow, Nora, some coincidence her escape route led her straight to the kitchen, a kitchen full of . . . weapons. Hmm, coincidence much? Next time, why not just have her drop into an armory and load up on machine guns? Try harder!

Where were all the kitchen workers while Scarlet was stealing knives and whittling down rolling pins into lethal stakes? Surely with fifty hungry vampires to feed, there must have been some hustling and bustling going on in that kitchen when she dropped in unannounced? I work as a waitress at the local diner part-time after school, and I can tell you the only time the kitchen is that empty is before we're open—or after we're closed.

How, if she hasn't been able to kill Count Victus in your first four books, will Scarlet Stain be able to kill him *and* forty-nine other equally powerful vampires at the same time?

How come you used the word *conclave* twelve times on the same page?

And you know what?

They'd be right.

My publisher doesn't understand why I can't just "whip out another Scarlet Stain" adventure, but . . . it's not so easy.

After four books, it's like I'm running out of plotlines, using too many coincidences to put the heroine of my books, Scarlet Stain, in just the right place at the right time.

Sure, it's easier on me, but these girls today are so sophisticated. They hop on those kinds of things in a hot minute.

For instance, in book three I made the mistake of introducing a new character to my Better off Bled series, a mysterious and (of course) handsome runaway who rescues Scarlet Stain from Count Victus in a weak moment.

That was all well and good, except that it just so happened this particularly mysterious and handsome runaway was a—wait for it—*zombie* who couldn't feel pain, who couldn't die, and who couldn't be turned into a vampire, and let me tell you . . .

Chicks.

Went.

Absolutely.

Vine-swinging.

Hair-pulling.

Fist-pumping.

Nuts!

They flocked to my book blog and called me a cheater, a phony, and threatened to never read another Scarlet Stain adventure again unless I killed off the character. I did, on the very first page of my next book.

At last they were happy, but that happiness came with a price (at least for me, anyway). Now it's like I'm too paralyzed to finish the book, afraid to make another mistake like that again. I sigh and look out the coffee shop window, where I see the sun has set (like, hours ago!).

I check my heart-shaped watch and curse under my breath.

If I don't skedaddle, *tout de suite*, I'm about to be late to yet another book signing.

I slide the cursed laptop into my messenger bag, nosh on the last wedge of stale biscotti that's been sitting unattended for the last few hours while I wrote my latest misguided scene, and toss the wrapper and my empty hot chocolate cup in the trash on my way out the door.

The evening air is crisp and cool this time of year, and I pull my jacket closer to my throat to keep out the chill.

My publisher, Hemoglobin Press (get it?), always makes sure to release the latest Better off Bled title in October, just in time for plenty of brisk sales before Halloween.

I check my watch again and do the mental math: the

Books 'n Beans megastore is on the corner of Maple Drive, which is two blocks away.

I can usually make it in ten minutes, walking at a comfortable pace, which is about all I can do with these stupid stiff black heels I always wear to these signings, but I have only eight minutes if I want to make it on time.

I shrug, pull the messenger bag closer for warmth, and settle on being fashionably late. (Hey, it's an author's prerogative.)

The heels click loudly on the pristine sidewalk of another spotless Beverly Hills side street, where I'm surrounded by clean trash cans and shiny No Parking at ANY Time signs every few steps.

During the day this street—more like an alley, really—would be bustling with Porsches and BMWs and all types of delivery vehicles, but now it's disturbingly deserted and all kinds of spooky.

Well, I shouldn't be surprised.

It's late for a school night, but the girls love these nighttime book signings, so as usual, I have to give the fans what they want.

Forget the fact that I've already put in a full day of school, done my homework *and* my laundry, and would love nothing more than to crash in my dorm suite and chill.

Not that I'm complaining, mind you. I couldn't afford to go to Nightshade Academy if it weren't for the fans.

The street is dim and quiet, with fall leaves blowing in the vacant road and crinkling underneath my scraping heels. I think, for the first time, that I should have walked the main drag, just to be under some better streetlamps and, you know, around other living people who might hear me shout if something bad actually happened.

This backstreet might be empty and cold, but it's the shortest route, and I *hate* to be late.

When I stop to adjust my messenger bag, I hear the footsteps. They stop moments later.

I turn, see nothing, and smile.

Ah, if only my fans could see me now, the horror writer spooked by the age-old Case of the Phantom Footsteps!

How many times have I written this very scene in one of my books, some thoughtless teenager walking carelessly down a deserted alley in some gritty city, being stalked by an unseen force that leaves—insert scary movie announcer voice here—*phantom footsteps*?

But this time it's different. I'm not some thoughtless teenager; I'm not exactly careless; this is a perfectly desirable street in the middle of Beverly Hills—pretty much the safest place on earth—and no one is stalking me. (I wish!)

But I could have sworn I heard the footsteps trying—and failing—to keep step with mine.

I quicken my steps and put my head down, eager to get back into civilization again.

I'm four minutes from Books 'n Beans when I hear the footsteps again.

This time I know they're there. The scraping is loud and not in sync with my own. But I don't turn around because whenever I do, there's a pause. There's no one standing there, let alone chasing me with arms out wide or a big butcher knife in each hand.

I head straight for the First National Bank at the corner of Maple and Elm, the big mirrored one with streetlights beaming down.

I force myself to walk slowly. I clutch the messenger bag

close to my side so it doesn't swish against my coat, hold my arms still so my coat won't rasp against my linen shirt.

I even hold my breath, trying to muffle my panic.

Now the only sound is my heels against the concrete.

And, of course, the footsteps of whoever is following me.

It's full dark out now, the street is deserted, and there's no one to help—no one around—if someone *is* following me.

I look left and see the bank's parking garage. I look ahead and see the megabookstore still too far away to be of any help.

But I can't look behind me for fear that someone will actually, you know, be *standing* there.

I finally reach the bank, smile at my reflection in the wall of mirrored glass—pause only slightly to stroke an auburn lock behind my ear—and walk briskly ahead.

The footsteps follow, but they must be echoes of my own shoes, because for the entire length of this humongous mirrored bank, I can see no one behind me.

No streaker in a long overcoat.

No escaped convict in orange prison scrubs.

No lunatic in a hockey mask with a chainsaw.

No Wolfman, no zombie, no mummy, no vampire on my tail.

Of course, a vampire—a *real* vampire—wouldn't cast a reflection, but . . .

*Come on, Nora. Seriously?*

*We're going there?*

*Really?*

*On the way to a book signing where you're going to be autographing copies of your new* vampire *book?*

*Irony much?*

I stand still, only to catch my breath. (I really need to get out from behind my laptop and move more often!)

Suddenly footsteps break the silence, heels on concrete forcing me to look back. This time I see a flash, a dark shape, moving quickly.

I look away too soon to see anything more, just that something is back there and gaining fast. So I run, something I haven't done in—gawd, who knows how long? I'm moving fast, sprinting in these stupid pumps and feeling awkward with my laptop bag slamming into my hips and the coat bunching up under my arms and the collar scratching my neck.

*Am I seriously doing this?*

*Running?*

*In the middle of Beverly Hills?*

But fear makes us do stupid things, such as look like a fool even in a world where YouTube exists and any number of fans could be shooting this right now, the harried author running from her own vivid imagination! (Idly I wonder how many hits something like this might actually get.)

Almost there now, almost, but not close enough to find safety in numbers. Anything could happen before help might arrive, all because I chose to spend the last two hours writing one more stupid page I'm never going to use in a book that I'll apparently never finish!

I start to breathe a sigh of relief when I finally see the alley behind Books 'n Beans just across the street, the back door already propped open and awaiting my arrival—they know me so well—when a hand grabs my elbow.

I whip around, messenger bag raised like a shield, room key up like a weapon. (Don't laugh. I saw it on *Dateline* once, or was it *20/20*?)

A plump teen waves a book in my face. "Nora?" she says, eyes wide as saucers. "Nora *Falcon*? Is it really *you*?"

I gasp, laugh, and sigh all in an instant.

What a dope I am!

I stop, stand still, feel a sudden thwacking sensation in my chest from too much exertion. I put my hands on my knees, catching my breath. All this time speeding up, slowing down, looking back, peering into mirrors, and I've been running from . . . a fan!

With eager hands, she shoves a copy of Better off Bled #4 at me.

I scramble for one of the six brand-new Sharpie pens in my bag.

"I can't believe it. My friends told me I was stupid, waiting around the corner for you to show up, but I know from that interview you gave in *Teen Talk* that you go to Nightshade Academy and your favorite coffee shop is the Hallowed Grounds, and I whipped out a map and figured, 'If she lives so close, she probably won't drive. Plus she's always talking about being a vegetarian, so that must mean she goes green, which probably means she doesn't even own a car, so . . . if she walks, this is the way she'd go!' And here you are! I can't believe it. My friends have been waiting in line for, like, hours to meet you. I just got here!"

"That's great detective work," I say, finally finding a Sharpie and pulling off the cap with my teeth.

"You think?" she asks, all braces and glasses and platinum-blonde curls.

I nod, holding the front flap of the book open with my pen poised.

"Gwendolyn," she says, already knowing the drill.

I write a short personal note, sign it with a flourish, and hand the book back. I'm so grateful she's not a mummy or a werewolf that I'd gladly buy her a lifetime supply of Scarlet Stain books instead of just signing the one.

She reads it, smiles, and kind of lingers there on the sidewalk, eager to chat.

I'd love to. Man, I would *much* rather stand on a dark backstreet and talk to one fan than sign books for three hundred, but duty calls.

"Are you coming to the store?" I ask, inching toward the back entrance and hoping she'll get the hint.

"Heck no." She laughs, already wise beyond her years. "That's for suckers! I already got my autograph. I'm heading straight for eBay!"

I frown, then laugh. "Well, off with you, then. I better get going and make sure your friends don't have to wait any longer."

"OK," she says.

I wave and start walking.

So does she. "Hey, I meant to ask," she says over her shoulder, clutching the book to her chest as she stands in the middle of the deserted street, "was that your boyfriend just now?"

"W-w-what? Huh?" My heart's suddenly pounding again. "When? Who?"

"You know," she says conspiratorially, "the hot guy behind you who disappeared the minute I showed up?"

# CHAPTER 1

There is one at every book signing.

I call them vannabes, short for vampire wannabes.

You know the type.

They're not just Goth; they're *way* Goth.

They don't merely read vampire books or watch vampire movies; they inhale them—lots of them, as many as their fake-contact-lensed eyes can endure.

They are allergic to the sun, to human boys, and apparently to modern fashion.

They dress as if they're out of an old *Dracula* movie, with frills and lace and pancake makeup and old hair combs.

I worry about them because they don't just like vampires; they want to *be* vampires. As in, literally, they want to feast on blood, live forever, have sharp teeth, and sleep by day, live by night—eternally. At least they *think* that's what they want, but they think they want it *more than anything.*

Some are young—too young to be reading my books (which can get a little racy and a *lot* violent, if I do say so myself), let alone be out past midnight at one of my standing-room-only book signings.

This one is roughly my age, seventeen or so, washed out, trembling in anticipation over meeting *the* Nora Falcon, author of the best-selling Better off Bled series featuring the fictional heroine Scarlet Stain, she of the flowing red locks, bodacious backside, and elite vampire-slaying legends.

"I can't believe it's *really* you." She squeals as she hands over the fourth and latest installment in the series, *Better Bled Than Dead*. "I've read all your books. This is by far the best!"

"Thank you," I say, hoarse from three straight hours of saying thank you. "That really means a lot to me . . ." I leave an intentional pause there at the end as the international sign for *Insert your name here*.

She blurts, "Anastasia," and averts her gaze.

"Anastasia." I sigh, pausing before committing it permanently to the inside jacket of the thick book I'm holding. "Is that your *real* name?"

"That's the name my coven gave me," she says somewhat self-consciously, looking to her left.

I follow her glance to a trio of identically dressed girls waving.

I wave back and murmur, "Some coven."

Anastasia says, "I know, right?"

And the way she says it, I can't tell if she's being self-deprecating or actually believes it's *some coven*.

"Maybe I should address this to your *real* name," I suggest, somewhat maternally, although we're clearly the same age. "You know, just in case you want to show it to your grandkids one day."

She takes a step back. "Well, why would I have grandkids?" she asks, snipping off each word like a tailor on a strict deadline cutting a hemline.

Uh-oh, she's not just a vannabe; she's a true believer. They're even worse. They believe vampires are real, and they hang out in covens and get dressed up and go to book signings at midnight.

"Well, you know, just in case you and your . . . coven over there grow up, get married, and have—"

"Grow up!"

Now her coven is no longer waving but looking like they're about to curse me from where they stand slurping frozen lattes in the bookstore café.

"Vampires never grow up. You of *all* people should know that, Nora Falcon!"

The bookstore security team—two bookish geeks barely older than me wearing mustard-yellow Books 'n Beans cashier aprons—look at us anxiously.

Really anxiously, as in, *We hope you know what to do in this situation, Nora, because one of us just wet his pants.*

I smile, wave, and nod to let them know I'm OK and turn my attention back to Anastasia. "Silly me," I say through clenched teeth. "Of course you're right, *Anastasia*."

She calms down a little as I make a big show of writing the following in her book:

*To Anastasia, a true believer, loyal fan, and beautiful soul.*

*All my best,*

*Nora Falcon*

She looks at it, sighs, harrumphs, and then holds it triumphantly over her head for her whole coven—all three of them—to see.

I reach for my second bottled water of the evening and turn to greet the next girl in line.

Only, it's not a girl—and he.

Is.

Hot.

Now, fair warning, I am *not* one of those girls who throw the word *hot* around loosely.

When you go to a school like Nightshade Preparatory Academy for Exemplary Boys and Girls in a place like Beverly Hills, well, hot guys are literally a dime a dozen.

I mean, these are guys who get paid to be hot: athletes, movie and TV stars, male models, that kind of thing.

These are the guys you see walking around half-naked in shaving cream commercials, wearing next to nothing in underwear ads, or leering at you from billboards as you drive to the mall.

So when I say this guy is hot, I mean hotter than hot. I mean *red* hot: flawless skin, high cheekbones, dark hair cut short—just right for an action figure.

"Uh, hi, um, helloooooo," I stammer and purr, and now it's my turn for trembling hands as I reach to grab the copy of *Better Bled Than Dead*.

He holds it just out of reach, making me look even more awkward as warmth creeps up my throat and into my cheeks.

"Can I just say," he oozes in a voice as smooth as caramel drizzling across a butter pecan sundae (both of which I could die for right about now, btw), "what an honor it is to meet Nora Falcon? *The* Nora Falcon."

"Please," I gush as he finally hands over the book. "I bet you say that to all the best-selling authors."

Ugh. Did I really just say that?

To *him*?

What a totally ridiculous thing to say to the first, and possibly only, hot guy to ever show up at one of my book signings.

I search his movie-star-handsome face for signs of revulsion and see only the darkest chocolate-brown eyes I've ever had the good fortune to peer into, live and in person. "Actually," he says, leaning in conspiratorially as a wisp of spicy cologne wafts pleasantly off his broad chest, "this is the first time I've ever been to one of these. But when I heard you'd be here tonight, I just couldn't resist."

I blush and open the book cover, and a piece of paper falls out. "Oops." I reach for it as it flutters onto the predictably black tablecloth the bookstore has used to cover up the fold-up picnic table I'm sitting at (you stay classy, Books 'n Beans), surrounded by towering stacks of my new book.

As I reach to hand it back, I take a peek and see it's a class schedule for none other than . . . Nightshade Academy.

What are the odds?

He reaches for it with long fingers tipped by manicured nails. "Sorry. I don't know *how* that got in there."

"That's crazy," I say, sitting up in my seat a little higher as all kinds of romantic possibilities flood my imagination and send my heart back into overdrive. "I go to Nightshade. Are you . . . new?"

He hangs his head a little, looks up at me with long lashes to match his heavenly eyes, and admits, "I just got into town, actually. I start at Nightshade tomorrow."

There follows a kind of awkward pause where I'm wondering whether to say something like *How nice* (too adult), *How awesome* (too trendy), or *How . . . appetizing* (too cheesy—unless it's coming out of the mouth of one of my characters, that is).

In the end, I don't say any of the above. I don't say anything at all. It's like my mind has short-circuited. It's like I'm so used to seeing girls at these things, chatting and smiling and feeling totally at ease without any testosterone in the room, and then this guy shows up and suddenly I'm out of my comfort zone in a major way.

Then he kind of blurts, "I'd love it if you could maybe, possibly, but no . . . that's too much to ask."

"What?" I ask, ignoring the dozen girls squirming in line behind Mr. Way-Too-Handsome-to-Be-at-a-Book-Signing Guy. "*What's* too much?"

"Nothing," he says, still avoiding eye contact, with his head hung low like a kid who's just broken his mom's favorite lamp and taped it back together and is waiting to get caught the next time she dusts. "It's just that, well, I'm new here in town and don't know anybody, and you know how it is your first day: it's make-or-break time, right? But if someone like *you* could show me around, just for a period or two, man, that would be awesome. See what I did there? I always do that; I meet someone new, find out we have something in common with each other, and then I overstep."

I shake my head, then nod too quickly, hurting my neck a little in the process. "Nonsense," I say, shooting a death glare at the vannabe tapping her foot behind Mr. Handsome. "I'd love to show you around. My locker's in D-wing. Just look for the one painted black—the freshmen think they're cute by doing that every year—and I'll be waiting for you. Now, I don't mean to be rude, but if I don't sign this and send you on your way, I'm afraid the mob behind you will have you roasting on a spit in five hot seconds."

"Oh, of course," he says. "Where are my manners? It's

Reece. Reece Rothchild, if you don't mind."

Reece.

Rothchild.

Seriously?

That's too rich.

He could be a character in one of my novels.

In fact, he should be in one of my novels! (Note to self: put Reece Rothchild in your next book.)

I write the following:

*To Reece, looking forward to an eventful school year.*

*Your new classmate,*

*Nora*

He pauses, reading it, before shutting the front cover slowly.

Immediately I'm editing it in my head: did I say too much, not enough?

Was I too friendly?

Too standoffish?

Too pushy?

He just stands there, not awkwardly, just . . . dazzlingly.

He is wearing jeans so fitted and custom washed, they must be expensive (perhaps even tailor-made), and black Venetian loafers so soft, you could spread them on a dinner roll, plus a gorgeous gray cashmere hoodie that hugs every inch of his rippling—

"Sorry," I blurt (too loudly!), suddenly realizing his thick, red lips have been moving—and apparently for quite some time now. "You were saying?"

He laughs gently, revealing straight white teeth. "Nothing much, Nora. I just said I'll see you tomorrow. D-wing, black locker, 7:15 a.m. sharp. I'm looking forward to it. Really."

When he says *really*, he nearly growls it, looking deep into my eyes.

I nod (me too!), watching as he makes a sharp left turn and exits the line, those long fingers running over my still-fresh inscription as if it were in Braille and he were reading it with his long, lingering fingertips instead of his luscious, dark-chocolate eyes.

He doesn't walk away so much as saunter, like a big cat in one of those documentaries about tigers in the jungle, his long legs moving him quickly through the bookstore as those skin-like jeans hug every curve of his tempting—

The next girl in line clears her throat forcibly.

I look up, blushing, to see a large girl with jet-black hair to match her voluminous cloak.

"Sorry, um . . ." I'm fishing for her name.

She smiles, hands over the book with predictably black-painted nails bitten to the quick, and announces, "Permafrost."

I still my hand before signing.

"Is that your *real* name?"

# CHAPTER 2

Abby is making ramen noodles in the dorm suite kitchen when I finally get home later that night.

Or should I say, early that morning.

I glance at the clock above the oven, and it says 1:14 a.m.

I wish I could say that either was a rare occurrence.

She has her imported French pore-opening mask on her angular face, but she's still in wardrobe from yet another night shoot—skuzzy black jeans and a faded rock-concert T-shirt covered in fake blood.

I yawn. "Did you just get *home*?"

She smiles in a thin line so as not to crack her mask and murmurs through pursed lips, "Ten minutes ago."

It comes out sounding like *Zen-mini-shee-go*, but we do this so often I now speak fluent face-mask-pinched-mouth-ese.

I look to the counter and see two thin-at-the-bottom, wider-at-the-top bowls, a set of shiny plastic chopsticks next to each. "You're making me some too?" I ask so hopefully it comes off as pathetic. I'm so hungry I could hug her! That is, if I didn't mind washing all that fake blood off my new linen shirt.

She nods, handing me the slotted spoon so I can take over while she washes off her mask in the communal bathroom.

I stir the noodles midboil, sighing at their close-to-perfect consistency. Leave it to Abby to stick me with the hardest part. I drain the noodles over the sink—we never eat them like soup but prefer them like lo mein—and split them up evenly into the two big bowls.

Abby has already put fresh chives, sesame seeds, soy sauce, steamed tofu chunks, and shaved ginger at the bottom of each bowl, so as the steam rises, it lets off a pleasantly pungent aroma that makes me feel right at home—not to mention downright ravenous.

She rushes in amid a cloud of fresh steam and something vaguely perfumy. She's freshly scrubbed and out of costume now, her long, lithe body still managing to look curvy in a pink nightshirt to match her fluffy slippers.

She flops down on the couch, and I join her.

"What a night!" she complains, then blows on her first chopstick full of still-steaming noodles. "Half the extras for the big zombie massacre we were shooting didn't show up, so we had to wait around for two hours while the assistant director went out and dragged thirty warm bodies in off the streets and got them in full wardrobe and makeup."

"What, you mean you had to sit in your four-thousand-square-foot trailer and wait two whole hours with your feet up while reading *Teen Talk*? There should be a march on the Hollywood Sign in protest!"

"Whatever." She sighs around a mouthful of steaming noodles. "Like your job's so hard, sitting around signing your John Hancock while a bunch of fans drool all over you. We should switch for a day and see how fun you think it is being a glamorous B-horror-movie star!"

"I'd love it," I snap, my noodles still too hot to eat and my stomach rumbling. "Then you can explain to my publisher why I won't be able to hit my next deadline."

"You *still* haven't started your next book?" she asks, sea-green eyes wide in mock shock. "You're always typing away on your laptop, so what are you writing if it's not about Satin Stain?"

"Uh, it's *Scarlet* Stain, and I am writing. All the time. It's just . . . nothing's really working for me, so I keep throwing it out."

"Still," she says around another mouthful, "it's not like you to miss a deadline. It's not like you to even come *close* to missing a deadline."

She looks at me disapprovingly over the lip of her bowl of steaming noodles.

"How can I make my deadline, what with book signings and homework and cooking you dinner every night?"

She smiles sarcastically, both of us too hungry to fake argue about our fake problems anymore.

Truth is, Abby looks as tired as I feel.

Joke around as I might, I know it's not easy going to class all day and filming the latest installment of her straight-to-DVD *Zombie Diaries* movie all afternoon and evening, plus most weekends.

I mean, it's one thing for me to sit around in the suite pecking away on my twenty-one-inch laptop cooking up new adventures for Scarlet Stain to endure, but Abby has to actually show up on set, looking good, lines rehearsed, and physically fight off fake zombies for hours every night.

OK, granted, she has plenty of downtime in that gargantuan trailer of hers on set, but even *that* can get old when you know you have to get your game face on any minute now.

"Why are you still on this shoot anyway, Abs? I thought it was supposed to last three weeks."

"It was." She groans, halfway through her noodles while I'm just starting mine. "But there were script problems, and they had to rewrite the ending, *again*, which means a few extra days of reshoots, and . . . do you care? Point is, we're going on week six, and I'm at my wits' end."

I smirk. "Well, you didn't have very far to—"

"Stuff it," she says before I can finish, mouth full, eyes smiling.

She sighs contentedly, somehow still managing to look pretty in her nightshirt now dotted with fresh ramen noodle stains. She's two inches taller than I am, maybe fifteen pounds lighter, and looks every bit the up-and-coming Hollywood starlet. She's not supermodel beautiful but only because she smiles so much, doesn't smoke, actually *eats*, and hasn't gotten any "work" done—yet. She is au naturel and still radiates perfection—damn her! As if that all wasn't more than enough, Abby also has that girl-next-door look, what with the chestnut-brown hair, sea-green eyes, pert button nose, and long, coltish legs.

She prances around the suite, doing the dishes, wiping down this, scrubbing off that, the bottom of her perfect butt poking out from under her nightshirt whenever she reaches too high—or bends too low. Not that I'm jealous or anything—heh—but what I wouldn't give to eat anything I wanted, all the time, and still look like a starlet.

I brush my teeth and get into my too-big nightshirt, and we're back in the suite, winding down for the night, morning, whatever, when Abby says, "Sooooo anything . . . interesting happen at your signing tonight?" She has a knowing look and a sly grin, neither of which I trust at the moment.

"Not really," I bluff.

I think vaguely of telling her about the phantom footsteps behind me on the way to the book signing, but she doesn't look like she's in the mood for anything serious right now. "At least, not unless you want to count the fact that every week now there are more and more true believers out there."

"Tell me about it," she says, and I know she's going to turn a question about me into yet another story about her. "Every night we get fans who insist they're zombies. As in, literally, the Living Dead. I honestly think some of them have even tried eating brains, like, for real. It's the craziest thing. It's like nobody wants to be *human* anymore!"

I nod, yawn, and rub my eyes.

"What I meant to say," she goes on, "is did *anyone* interesting show up to your signing tonight?"

I think of Reece Rothchild, he of the chocolate-brown eyes and snug jeans. I try to hide my blush and fail epically. "What are you up to, Abs? It's too late to play your reindeer games."

"There's this thing called the Internet," she explains, her pink slippers up on the coffee table as she pins me with those green eyes, "and people who use the Internet have these things called websites. Even companies like, oh, say, the local Books 'n Beans on the corner there? And, well, *some* of these bookstores—I'm not saying which ones, now—have these things called live cams, and certain actresses, who shall remain nameless for obvious reasons, when they are stuck in their *two*-thousand-square-foot trailers, not *four*-thousand-square-foot trailers, waiting for the AD to round up thirty zombie extras, can click on these webcams and watch their roommate totally flirt with some hot guy in a gray cashmere hoodie that looked like it was *totally* made for him. You know, somewhere in France! So, I'll ask you again, did—?"

"First of all, stalk much? And second, yes, a hot guy *did* show up to my book signing tonight, and I *was* going to tell you about it—eventually—but my mouth was full of ramen, and it's late, and I figured you talk to hot guys every day of your glamorous movie-star life, so why would *you* be interested if I talk to one for all of two-point-three minutes?"

She rolls her eyes, then waits out a yawn from yours truly. "Hmm, why would I be interested that my best friend and roommate—who has taken a vow of celibacy ever since she got her heart broken by that hunky snowboarder her sophomore year—would be talking to the hottest guy to ever show up to one of her signings? Hmm, I wonder, Nora. Why do *you* think, hm?"

"OK, for one, that snowboarder didn't break my heart. And two, I haven't taken a vow of celibacy. It just . . . kind of turned out that way through *no* fault of my own. And three, how would you know *how* many hot guys show up at my signings since you've never even come to one? Ever?"

She sits up. "Well, I'm sorry if I'm too busy out shooting movies in order to buy ramen noodles to feed *you* when you come back from your signings to actually go to one!"

I snort and throw a silk pillow at her.

We both know we're being ridiculous, but despite the late hour, it's too fun to stop. Besides, there are plenty of throw pillows to go around. The school provided us with furniture in each of the two-room dorm suites, but of course Abby and I weren't happy with the suede-and-polyester sectional number they gave us when we first moved in, so we had to redecorate. Silk throw pillows—not to mention a matching couch and love seat combo—were our first step. Matching silk curtains, a fireplace unit—for our silk Christmas stockings, natch—oriental end tables, and lots of earthen bowls with beaded balls (Abby's fave accessory) followed.

Now the dorm suite is a stylish affair and our favorite place to hang—that is, when we're not at signings or on movie sets or in class or at the gym or . . .

"Hey," she says, out of throw pillows now and eager to get back to basics. "*Paperback vriter*. What about this hot mystery man you were talking about?"

"I'm tired," I say, ignoring Abby's use of her favorite term for me, a dig on my chosen specialty in fang fiction. "I'll tell you all about Reece tomorrow. In fact, you can meet him, if you want."

Now she's really sitting up.

"Whoa, wait, you're not going anywhere until you dish this-here dirt. Reece? Tomorrow? You know his name *and* you're seeing him again? When did you, of all people, become a player? What gives, sister?"

"You'll be seeing him too. That is, if I can ever get you up in the morning. He's going here now, to Nightshade. Starts tomorrow, in fact. His freshly printed schedule was in his book, and when I went to sign it, it slipped out, and I saw that he was—"

"Ah, this guy is slick." She smiles, kicking my feet off the coffee table for emphasis. "You think he just happened to show up and just happened to hand you a book to sign with his schedule inside?"

"Yeah, sure," I mutter, almost defensively. "It happens all the time."

"Really, Nora, when was the last time it happened? Tell me, quickly!"

"OK, never, but . . . it didn't *look* staged, if that's what you're implying."

"So it didn't look staged. That just means he's really, really good at it."

She looks at me funny, like a troop leader checks out the Girl Scout who sold the most boxes of cookies when he didn't think she had it in her. "Nora, you might just have your first stalker."

"Stalker. Yeah right. I *wish* someone cared enough about me to track me down, find out what school I attend, register there, print out his schedule, buy one of my books, come to one of my signings, slip his schedule into the book, and hand it to me just so we'd have something to talk about for two-point-three minutes."

Hm, what's that I tell my vannabes at every book signing?

Be careful what you wish for.

Yeah, if only I'd thought of that before I agreed to meet Reece at my locker the next morning.

# CHAPTER 3

For the record, Reece never shows up at my locker the next morning.

He never shows up at my locker at all.

Instead he shows up in homeroom, bearing flowers and chocolates, and literally gets down on one knee to apologize.

Yeah, OK, I know I'm a writer, but I am seriously *not* making this up.

But wait, let me back up a bit and break it down for you.

So I got here bright and early, really early, because I'm not used to meeting hot guys at my locker.

Heck, I'm not used to meeting *any* guys at my locker.

OK, maybe Wyatt Cash, but he's different. (And in a *very* good way.)

And I'm there, at like 6:45—even though Abby warns me to play hard-to-get and arrive after 7:16—and I'm dressed, well . . . elegantly.

For me, anyway.

Typically I shlub through my days as much as possible. There's no uniform at Nightshade Preparatory Academy for

Exemplary Boys and Girls (yes, it actually does say that on our school sign, thank you very much), so typically I just do the baggy jeans, (mostly) clean T-shirt, and hoodie look. But today Abby swore she wouldn't let me out of the dorm suite in anything less than business casual, so I had to look through my closet for something a little more appropriate.

Only when I was in snug black linen slacks, a white cotton turtleneck, and wobbling around on unfamiliar—to say nothing of uncomfortable—black heels did she let me leave the room, and only then when she'd grabbed a bright red satin scarf from one of the many pegs on her wall and cinched it tight around my waist.

So there I stand, reeking of Abby's imported French perfume, looking ridiculous next to my black-painted locker from 6:45 to 6:50 to 6:55 to 7:00.

I get excited around the 7:03 mark as I see the crowd in the commons area part for a staggeringly handsome teen.

But then I recognize my other best friend, Wyatt Cash, strolling up. As usual, his appearance makes my heart race in a very romance novel way, though by now I've learned to control the sudden blush that used to creep into my cheeks every time he appeared. To say nothing of the thumping of my heart or the soft, rosy glow in the pit of my stomach. I look at him, his hair close-cropped, his jaw square, his eyes a shimmering blue. He's looking athletic, as always, in a sleek white tracksuit that is so *wow, that's so retro-hip it's cool again* it must have been a gift from one of the sportswear companies he frequently models for.

"Nora!" he says, clearly surprised to see me loitering at my locker so close to the first homeroom bell. "Aren't you afraid you'll get an almost demerit if you get to homeroom only ten minutes early?"

I slug his shoulder. "Where'd you get the new duds?"

He flips the jacket collar, striking a pose as he replies, "I just did a gig for this new European sportswear company. This is their latest. Dig it?"

"Very sporty," I say, forcing myself not to look for Reece over Wyatt's broad shoulder. "Look out—you could start a new trend."

"If I'm lucky. Hey, listen. Sorry I couldn't make it to your signing last night, but . . . something came up."

"Oh yeah?" I ask, slugging him again. (Man, his biceps are hard!) "What was her name?"

"Very funny." He leans against the locker next to mine. "Turns out they needed some extras on Abby's new flick last night, so I figured, this could be my big break, right? Who knew I'd be buried under three pounds of zombie makeup, but Abs promised I'd get my name in the credits, so at least it will be good for my reel, right?"

My cheeks flush with sudden, irrational jealousy. "Absolutely. Abby told me they needed extras, but she didn't mention she'd made a special request for male models to show up." I try to keep the resentment out of my voice.

Wyatt shrugs. "Yeah, well, she probably just didn't want you to know she was the reason I couldn't make it to your signing. So how'd it go?"

I shrug back. "It went just like all the other book signings you and Abby can never make it to."

He laughs again, his teeth pearly white but charmingly crooked, like his smile and sense of humor. "You know none of us male models can read. What if I do show up and someone picks on me and asks me to read a passage out loud?"

"I guess I should thank you," I say, my heart fluttering as I catch sight of Reece over Wyatt's shoulder . . .

Nope, no, false alarm. Just that tall kid from the deodorant commercials.

"If you ever were to come to one of my signings, the girls would all mob you, and I'd be left alone at my little table, signing my name on the tablecloth in despair."

"Who are you looking for?" One of his eyebrows arch; the other one, too.

"What? Who? Nobody. Why?"

"Nora, you are the worst liar. If I didn't know better, I'd swear you were waiting here for someone. Oops, there's second bell. He better hurry up, or you'll be late—for once."

And with that he is off, racing down the commons toward the gym for his first—of three—gym classes of the day.

I loiter for a few minutes more, until the very last second before I really will be late for homeroom.

I make it just in time, grabbing my usual seat next to Abby and settling in with a *Don't even go there* face.

For once, she doesn't.

But Bianca Ridley does, tapping the back of my seat with her garishly jewel-encrusted—and ridiculously expensive—heels. "Look who's suddenly gunning for Most Likely to Play Dress-Up, girls."

Abby turns around and shoots her a look, but I choose to ignore her (as usual).

Meanwhile her posse, a group of similarly entitled, well-to-do chicks with fake smiles and even faker tans, all giggle.

"Needs a little more work," one of them not-so-quietly mutters.

"I'll say," murmurs another.

My face burns, and Abby looks at me expectantly, probably waiting for me to whip up one of my trademark comebacks.

It's at this precise moment that Reece Rothchild knocked on the door.

Yes, he knocked.

Not once but twice!

So of course Mrs. Armbruster, our exceedingly nice but dangerously narcoleptic homeroom teacher, has to get up from drooling all over the roll book—hm, guess I could have hung out by my locker a little longer—and ever so slowly walks to the door.

By the time she gets there, a full thirty seconds later—I'm timing it on the black-and-white clock above her desk—of course the class is anticipating who it might be.

Principal Chalmers, there to pluck some unlucky student out for detention?

A singing telegram?

A UPS guy in short shorts with another box of organic, gluten-free breakfast bars for Bianca?

A flower delivery guy, also in short shorts, also for Bianca?

When the door finally opens, lo and behold, Reece stands there.

Suddenly, like, six of the eight girls in the room openly gasp in admiration. (Yeah, I'm one of them. What of it?)

"Who's the hunk?" asks Bianca.

"I don't know," says one of her minions, "but as soon as I find out, I'll be writing his name on my folder three thousand times today; that's for sure."

Abby looks over, likely sees the blush creeping above my suddenly cloying turtleneck collar, and whispers, "Your boy sure knows how to make an entrance!"

Does he ever. Today he's wearing wheat-colored cords and a faded off-white rugby shirt with maroon sleeves and a matching collar, which is unbuttoned just enough to reveal the hint of his bulging pecs but not quite enough to say *tool*. His sneakers are impeccably—and purposefully—distressed, much like the satchel clinging to one broad shoulder.

"May I?" Reece asks, a bouquet of long-stemmed roses in one hand, a brown velvet (velvet?) box of chocolates in the other.

"May you what, dear?" Mrs. Armbruster says with obvious glee, the color rising to her own cheeks.

"Enter, madam?" he says with equal good humor.

"Please do," she says, making a grand, sweeping gesture of standing off to the side.

Reece spots me in the middle of the next-to-last row and strides over. He looks at no one else in the room, not a soul. Not at Abby, who is gorgeous (and famous). Not at Bianca, who is even gorgeouser (though slightly less famous). Not even at the tramps who flank Bianca, who are not quite as pretty but doubly trampy and well worth ogling.

Instead he focuses those dark-chocolate eyes like a laser beam on me and, just before getting to my desk, goes to one knee, and presents the flowers and chocolates. "Allow me to apologize for my tardiness at your locker this morning, Nora. Some . . . unforeseen circumstances prevented me from getting there on time."

"Reece, I-I-I—" I try, until at last I take his offerings and lay them on my desk.

Only then does he stand, grabbing something out of his front pocket, and just when I let myself think it's going to be some kind of diamond-slathered engagement ring (greedy much?), he turns on his heel and walks away to hand his schedule to Mrs. Armbruster.

"Reece Rothchild," he says, his cheeks dimpling. "Reporting

for duty, ma'am."

"I'd say." Mrs. Armbruster wheezes as she gathers up the bifocals resting comfortably on her massive chest and slides them on her nose. "Take a seat, Reece, if you will."

He does so, right next to me.

I sit there like a pity prom date, suffocating in my turtleneck, about to bust out of my black slacks—which I bought for a chorus recital freshman year and haven't worn since—and literally watching my nose grow three sizes as the roses in such close proximity cause my sinuses to swell.

Once Mrs. Armbruster has duly recorded his name in the roll book and handed back his schedule, she promptly returns to her desk and—naps out.

Reece looks from her to me with amusement. "Is she always this . . . attentive?"

I snort, and Abby goes to extraordinary lengths to elbow me from one desk over, causing me to double-snort.

"Uh, Reece, this is my best friend, Abby—"

"Abby Hastings," Reece finishes for me, reaching across my desk to shake her hand. "I'd know that face anywhere. I'm a big fan of *Zombie Diaries*. I've got the first four on Blu-ray. We used to watch them all the time at my old school."

"Oh yeah?" Abby opens the big brown velvet box of chocolates on my desk minus an invitation. "Where's that?"

"Milton Prep in Manhattan. My . . . elders thought it was time for a change of pace, so here I am."

"Well, it's awfully nice to meet you," she says around a gorgeous dark-chocolate truffle. "Remind me, and I'll get you the fifth *Zombie Diaries* on Blu-ray. It's not even out yet, but for you, I'll make an exception."

"Thanks," he says as she heads next to a white-chocolate

crème that starts melting before it's even crossed the threshold of her lips.

"Those look really good," I say to Reece, leaning forward a smidge so he won't see my best friend devouring most of the boxful. "You really didn't have to go to so much trouble. I mean, I understand about you being late."

Then I see the tag on the flowers—Beverly Hills Bouquet Emporium—and realize it's halfway across town. "Although it sure seems like if you'd gone someplace a little closer to campus to get the flowers, you might have gotten here on time."

"Ah, an eye for the details. Well, what else should I expect from an author of such . . . caliber? I admit, I might have suspected I'd be late and made a few pit stops just in case."

"Well, either way, it was really way too generous."

"Yeah," comes a voice from behind. "From what I hear, a used piece of bubble gum would have been all it takes to impress Nora."

Abby gasps and probably would have snatched a handful of Bianca's hair if she hadn't been in a chocolate coma.

I do what I always do—ignore Bianca—despite my mortification.

To my relief, Reece also acts as if he hasn't heard. "I hope the offer to show me around school still stands, Nora."

Bianca says, "Sure, fine, if you want the nickel tour. I'll be glad to give you the platinum version, Reece."

I watch as Reece's face slowly . . . changes.

He's still smiling, but now the lips look thin, the expression vaguely . . . cruel. He turns. "I'm sorry. I didn't catch your name."

"Bianca Ridley, as in Ridley's Department Stores, forty-five hundred and counting across the US, Europe, and Asia."

"I see. So you're here because of your father's accomplishments then?"

For once Bianca's porcelain-doll face looks like it's about to crack. "Well, sure, aren't we all?"

"Well, not quite. Abby, it would seem, is here because of her acting ability. Nora is here because of her writing ability. Why would I want someone who can't do anything for herself to show me around a school full of overachievers?"

As if on cue, the bell rings, and Abby and I stand quickly to avoid further incident. We linger at the door as the crowd floods past.

Meanwhile, Reece stands in front of Bianca, who's still seated, as if he's about to toss her desk across the room.

"Reece?" I ask, trying not to sound desperate.

"In a minute, Nora," he says. "Bianca and I aren't quite through yet. You run along, and I'll catch up. Promise."

And still we wait as Bianca rises.

She is alone now, her entourage having known when to make themselves disappear.

On her $760 heels, she is nearly Reece's height, but his glower makes him somewhat larger than life.

I say, "OK," hoping my voice will snap him out of it, but he barely glances my way.

Abby and I turn, and the minute we're out the doorway, it slams shut all by itself, as if Nightshade Academy is suddenly . . . haunted.

Back in the hallway, we stow the flowers and candy in Abby's locker because, let's face it, I'm allergic to the first and she's halfway through the other.

"What was *that* all about?"

"I don't know," I say, grabbing my AP English book, "but

I'd love to be a fly on the wall."

Abby chews her lips as she walks with me to our next class. "I dunno," she says dubiously, avoiding eye contact. "Looked like a lot of sexual tension there, if you know what I mean."

"No," I snap before considering it. Then: "Really? You think?"

"I don't know." She sighs, slowing down to let a group of obnoxious freshmen pass. "I hope not. If he was stalking *you*, he should have better taste than *that*."

I nod. "I mean, I wouldn't put it past her."

"Well, you and Bianca have a history, after all."

"I'd hardly call it a history." I laugh as we head down D-wing.

"She stole that stupid snowboarder from you. You don't consider that history?"

"OK, for one, she didn't *steal* him; I just happened to break up with him the same day they started dating."

"I would hardly call making out in the detention room *dating*, but if you want to live in your fictional world, I guess I can't blame you."

"What?" I say as we finally enter AP English together, sliding into our seats, again near the back of the room. "What does *that* mean?"

"It means," she whispers, "you tend to create these stories for yourself, and not just in your books."

"Like what stories?" I struggle to keep my voice down.

A few kids up front slide their chairs back ever so slightly to eavesdrop.

"Like your snowboarder dude story. He did too break up with you first, because Bianca seduced him. I'm sorry, but that's the truth." I know it's the truth. Does she think I don't know that? That I don't remember it? The months and months of kicking myself for not seeing the signs earlier, and then the months and months after that, pining for the guy even though I knew how pitiful it looked?

And how little he cared?

I shake my head until I can't deny it any longer, then murmur, "So, what, you think history is repeating itself?"

"We'll see," she says.

"And pretty soon," I add, nodding toward the door.

After all, I couldn't help but notice on his schedule that both Bianca and Reece share this class with us. We watch the door in silence, waiting for them to appear. We're not the only ones; Bianca's posse sit in the very back row, awaiting their lord and master.

Second bell rings and Mr. Richards appears, looking fresh-faced and handsome, as always.

Abby gives him a special smile, and I return my focus to the doorway.

A few last-minute stragglers come in, none of them as shockingly handsome as either Bianca or Reece.

By the time third bell rings, Abby is holding my hand. Two minutes later I know in my heart that history *is* repeating itself, after all. They're not coming to class. They're probably skipping right now, heading for the nearest cheap hotel to rip each other's clothes off and do who knows what to each other, Lord knows how many times, before curfew tonight.

I shake my head.

Abby "tsk-tsks" in her told-you-so voice. Who can blame her? She's right, after all. Bianca *has* stolen another man from me, and this time it took only one period.

# CHAPTER 4

"So, I don't get it," says Wyatt, peering into the dorm-size fridge under our sink after school that day. "The guy shows up at your book signing last night, asks for your autograph—smooth move, by the way; I need to add that to the Wyatt Repertoire—*begs* you to show him around school the next day, shows up late, showers you with affection, gives you flowers you can't smell and candy you can't eat, gets into it with Bianca over your honor, and then . . . disappears? With that snooty Bianca, of all people?"

He emerges triumphantly with the last diet soda, pops the top before asking if I want any (or even if he can have any), and plops down on the love seat opposite the couch. I wonder if he knows, if he has a single inkling, how much I like it when he's around, and how much it would mean if he noticed—just once.

"Pretty much," I say.

He flinches. "I've heard of playing hard to get, but either the dude's got mad skills or he's just . . . flaky. I mean, you? Bianca? It's apples and oranges. He needs to make up his mind whether he wants ground chuck or filet mignon, you know what I mean?"

"That depends." I smile, just shy of flirting. "Am I the ground chuck in this story? Or the filet mignon?"

"What do you think?" He laughs over his half-finished soda and, in typical Wyatt style, neither confirms nor denies his answer. "Either way, are you sure this guy's for you?"

"What do you mean *for me,* Wyatt? It's not like we're promised to each other or anything. I was just venting; that's all. Forget I said anything."

Wyatt eyes me coolly over the shiny silver soda can. "Whoa, easy there. What else should I think? I mean, I stop by for a casual social visit, you're pining away, and the first thing out of your mouth is this tirade about some guy named Reece—that's a fake name if ever I've heard one, by the way, and I'm a model, so I should know—and you expect me to think you're *not* interested in the guy?"

I can't tell if he's mad, bored, jealous, or all three. That's the problem with Wyatt; those endless blue eyes hide all his secrets.

I sigh. "I'm not sure if I'm interested. I mean, maybe I am. I just . . . When did Abby say she'd get back?"

He pulls a cell phone from his jacket, scrolls until he finds her text, and reads it for me: "Another late shoot, no extras needed, working on that screen credit for you. Tell Nora I'll be home after dinner."

He looks at me skeptically. "What, you'd rather talk about this with her?"

"Yeah, frankly," I snap.

He's used to it by now. That's what he gets for being a BFF to two FFs (frustrating females).

"Look, I can relate as good as Abby does," he says.

"As *well* as Abby does," I correct, not really meaning to.

A bad habit.

"Whatever. I'm saying, I saw *He's Just Not That Into You*. I'm down. I'm hip."

"You are down, you are hip, you *have* seen *He's Just Not That Into You*, but you're still a player, and you can't relate to someone—especially a girl—who isn't."

"A player? Me? Please." He crumples the empty soda can and tosses it—for a miss—toward the half-size trash can under the sink.

"Wyatt, please, you've dated three models, two of them super-, twelve starlets, including Abby for two months last year, four girls from the Swedish volleyball team—two at the same time—so how are you *not* a player?"

"Please. Most of those were publicity stunts. Four of the starlets were gay, the models were airheads, the volleyball girls I'll give you, but can you blame me?"

"Not really," I concede, trying to remain impartial even though every cell in my body seethes with jealousy. "I guess it's hard *not* to get dates when you're posing half-naked on a billboard at Sunset Boulevard."

"Exactly. Those girls don't want me; they want the image of me they see in magazines or whatnot."

His jacket is open, the white T-shirt underneath stretched across his pecs and six-pack abs as if it were designed especially for him. For all I know, it could have been.

The problem with a place like Nightshade Academy is there are no average-looking people to commiserate with. Seriously, people think my life is glamorous because of the books, but at the end of the day, I'm just another mousy book-worm tapping away at the keys behind the scenes while Abby and Wyatt are in front of the camera, smiling and seducing people all over the world.

There are very few people here who *aren't* traffic-stoppingly beautiful. Even the do-nothing celebs like Bianca and her minions are gorgeous, as if their genes know they're rich and respond accordingly.

You walk through the halls, and it's like you've just shown up at an audition for *America's Top Model.* You meander through the cafeteria line with a few bowls of mac and cheese, and the anorexics all look at you like you're feeding on live cats or something!

"You wouldn't understand," I hear myself grumbling.

"Try me," Wyatt says, giving me his best *I'm listening* smile.

As usual, I fall for it.

As usual, he doesn't let me down.

Here's the thing about Wyatt: beautiful as he is, I would still crush hard on him even if he looked like Elmer Fudd, because he's just a solid, righteous dude. He's the kind of guy who doesn't just become your friend but literally wedges his way into your life. He just shows up, expecting to be charming and actually *being* charming. Like popping into the dorm suite unannounced, no knocking, just, "Hey, ladies, here I am!" Or the way he texts you all day long with funny stories about classmates or teachers, or the way he remembers your birthday—OK, four days late despite about half a dozen social media alerts, but still—with half-price coconut Easter eggs because your birthday is April 12 and you can't be mad at him, ever, because who else remembers coconut is your favorite?

Even Abby mixes it up and always gets me crème eggs, which are just gross, but I have to eat them anyway because she's so proud she thinks she's remembered my favorite.

Is it any wonder I've been secretly in love with the guy

since, like, the first day I met him?

It was right after new student orientation, and I'd just come from my counselor's office, loaded down with paperwork and rule books and the keys to my suite. I was already a freshman transplanted from my little Florida surf town, intimidated by this famous school that accepts only "exceptional boys and girls"—exceptionally *beautiful* boys and girls, from what I'd just seen walking across campus. And so what do I find when I step off the elevator on my very first day at Nightshade Academy but a dark-haired god asleep on the floor outside his dorm suite door.

And why is he passed out two doors from mine?

Only because he left his keys at some supermodel's house (of course) the night before and is locked out.

He was still in his party clothes that morning: tight gray jeans and a black shirt unbuttoned to his navel, and although I'd never even met my future roommate, Abby, I let him sleep it off on our (old) couch.

When she finally got up and saw him lying there, she rolled her eyes and warned, "Don't fall in love with him, Nora. He's the nicest guy who'll ever break your heart."

She'd been right, of course, but not too right to fall in love with him herself. It didn't last long, and it's not something any of us talk about much anymore, but the brief romance between my two BFFs is the elephant in every room—even if I'm the only one who still feels its crushing weight every time I see their knowing glances from across the room.

Now we both call him our best friend, even though we'd each agree to marry him—or fight to the death trying—if he ever even got close to bending on one knee.

For any reason.

I'm talking to pick up a piece of trash from the floor!

"I just—it's confusing," I say. "He acts like he's all into me one minute. Showing up at my book signing like that, letting me see his schedule, begging me to show him around school. Flowers and chocolates. Then he dumps me."

"Guys do that. It's all part of the game."

"*I* don't play those games."

"That's why you haven't been on a date since that stupid snowboarder broke your heart."

"He *didn't* break my heart, OK? What is it with everybody? I got emotionally attached, he's in love with his stupid board and his money and his Xbox and anything in a short skirt—or preferably *no* skirt—so we very maturely decided to go our separate ways."

He smirks. "Ah, so *that's* why you made the bad guy in your very next book a snowboarder. Because you're sooooo mature."

I toss a silk throw pillow at his almost concave stomach. "So you *do* read my books?"

He puts one long, tan finger to his full lips. "Shhh, don't tell anyone, or you'll damage my street cred."

"On what street do you have cred, Wyatt? Besides Rodeo Drive."

He shrugs, grabs the bag of corn chips from the coffee table, counts out three, and chews them carefully while eyeing me from his love seat.

"Nora, obviously this guy wants something from you. The schedule-in-the-book trick? Classic come-on. You're just too insecure to realize it. So that didn't work, and he upped his game with the chocolates-and-flowers trick. Hey, just 'cause Bianca caused him to lose his mojo doesn't mean he's not still into you."

"So then where did he go all day? And where was Bianca? You know her—she'd rather eat her arm than miss a minute of school. Nightshade is like her own personal catwalk. The only way she would miss is if some hot new guy convinced her to play hooky."

"I don't think they call it hooky anymore. I think it's called ditching now."

"Who cares?"

"Well, as a writer, I figure you'd want to pay attention to those kinds of details."

"The only details I want right now are what happened between Bianca and Reece all day."

"You sure about that?" he asks, looking at his watch.

"No. Not really."

# CHAPTER 5

*Scarlet Stain holds on to the fire escape railing, one trembling hand clutching the cold, hard steel of the ladder and the other gripping her sword. Count Victus's blood is still fresh and drips off the sharp blade to the darkened alley six stories below.*

*From above comes the rustling of what she knows to be a black satin cape, its edges curling around the count's ankles as he hovers just out of reach.*

*"I don't know why you won't let me turn you, dear." He sighs, warm breath oozing like a summer breeze across the otherwise frigid night. It splashes Scarlet's cheeks like an almost welcome embrace. "Life, or should I say the afterlife, would be so much . . . simpler."*

*Then he bares his fangs, so glistening and white, his lips still red and raw from gorging on his latest victim, another innocent Scarlet pledged and failed to protect.*

*As he covers the distance between them, eyes piercing, Scarlet has only one escape: straight down. She lets go of the fire escape, so quickly that even the count, with all his miraculously immortal superpowers, can't stop her.*

*Nor, curiously, does he try.*

*She falls, the weight of the world on her shoulders, rushing her speedily toward the earth. Not even the count can save her now.*

*That is, if he even wanted to . . .*

I hit Save and look away from the keyboard, rubbing my eyes with one hand as I reach for my coffee cup with the other.

Around me the bright café is bustling, the smells of freshly brewed cappuccino, frothy milk, hot chai tea, and nutmeg filling the air. The hum of informed, energetic conversation trills from most tables, while the rest feature solitary keyboard-tapping caffeine jockeys like me.

I always come to the Hallowed Grounds café when it's time to write another chapter. My room is too small, and the dorm suite phone is always ringing if Abby's not there, or she's gabbing on it if she is.

Here I'm not Nora Falcon, best-selling author, but just another anonymous face bathed in the blue glow from my laptop monitor. Here I can be anyone I want to be. A high school senior, filling out applications for Harvard or Yale. A sexy (OK, not-so-sexy) single, writing up my profile for some online dating site. An irate customer, shooting off a profanity-laced complaint to the Hallowed Grounds corporate website. Or, considering my 90210 zip code, just another struggling writer, typing up a screenplay between waitressing gigs.

I enjoy the anonymity while nibbling on an almond biscotti and searching for the next scene.

I have no idea what's going to happen to Scarlet now that she's falling through the air with no net or hero to save her.

That's just the problem. I never do.

Either I'll figure out a way for her to survive the fall just before she lands in the wet, smelly alley below—or I'll go back and do a rewrite.

Unfortunately, I've been doing more rewriting than writing lately, which could be why my publisher keeps hounding me to deliver the fifth installment in the Better off Bled series.

I stare at the half-empty page, envious of the other writers scattered around me; their fingers seem to always be flying, their heads always down, writing with purpose and passion.

The way I used to do.

Back then I'd been just another vannabe, a freshman in Barracuda Bay High School, entering writing contest after writing contest with my crazy stories about Scarlet Stain and her archenemy, the evil vampire Count Victus.

We didn't have a computer at home (insert commiserating *aw*s here), so I'd get to school early, stay late, and even eat lunch in front of my favorite monitor in the computer lab: the last one all the way to the right.

I'd type and type and type and type. The lab administrator in his glass-walled office, a plump guy by the name of Mr. Mason, would shake his head in marvel as he downed another donut.

Nothing came of it, not a penny, not a ribbon, not a prize, until one day I got a call from the folks at Hemoglobin Press, *the* premiere publisher of fang fiction, otherwise known as vampire literature.

Months earlier I'd entered one of their contests, overlooking the fact that the first prize was a book contract from the publisher—and never in a million years expected to win.

But I *did* win, and everything changed.

Practically overnight.

Months later the first Scarlet Stain book was published.

It took off like fresh hotcakes on a winter morning, and the rest is history.

My mom, a struggling waitress at the time, had heard about Nightshade Academy in one of her gossip magazines—that all the stars' kids and all the smart and talented and beautiful kids went there. She was convinced that it was the right place for a girl like me.

So after I made enough from the first Better off Bled book to get her out of the trailer park and into a big house in the nicest part of town, she signed me up and shipped me off.

That was freshman year, and I haven't been home since. The feeling I get from Mom and her new husband, Ronald, is that they'd rather see my monthly checks than little old me.

Fine by me.

Mom always said I was "just another mouth to feed" anyway; now I can feed Ronald and her via long distance, and everyone—including me—is happy.

But along with the very adult freedoms of making my own money and living away from home with all the beautiful people at Nightshade Academy came very adult pressure: the need to achieve, to keep up with a grueling publication schedule of two new books a year, plus a full course load, the rare extracurricular activities I'd need if I decided I wanted to get into a good college, and the normal social life of being a semipopular teenager in a place like Beverly Hills.

Sometimes it's heaven. I mean, who am I to complain, right?

Other times it's hell.

Right now I'm somewhere in between.

I sigh, polish off my first biscotti in frustration, and contemplate another when the bell over the door chimes.

I look to see who it might be—in this town, you never know when a Taylor or a Vin or a Kanye or even a Kim might stop in for a quick pick-me-up—when instead I see . . . Reece.

He has changed again, this time into black track pants, expensive sneakers, and a shiny silver hoodie, the kind you might wear while running a marathon—on the moon!—and walks straight to my cozy corner table.

He's so confident, so smooth, like a predator on the hunt. Is it any wonder my heart skips a beat and he is instantly forgiven?

I try to look away, to act bored, or at least disinterested, and fail miserably.

Does he act so confident because I'm desperate?

Or am I desperate because he acts so confident?

I close my laptop out of habit. I hate anyone, no matter how beautiful, reading my work until it's finished, polished, and printed.

And even then, I prefer they do it as far away from me as humanly possible.

"Nora," he says, taking a seat across from me. "I am so sorry."

"Are you, like, bipolar?" I somehow find the courage to ask before he can make himself comfortable.

He doesn't smile. "No, I don't think so. Why do you ask?"

I look at him in amazement.

Is he that cold?

Or just that clueless?

"Dude." I lean in just a tad so we don't become a spectacle for the rest of the Hallowed Grounds patrons. "You have stood me up twice, brought me chocolates and roses, and now you've tracked me down to my favorite café—all in less than twenty-four hours. It's like you're Jekyll and Hyde or something."

"Wrong book," he murmurs. Before I can fake a coughing fit and ask him, *Dillweed says what?* he adds, "It was unforgivable, but I must ask, *can* you forgive me?"

I shake my head, too tired to play these games. "I don't *want* to forgive you. We don't know each other well enough for forgiveness at this point. What I'd like is for you to either quit doing things I *need* to forgive or just . . . leave me alone."

He arches one eyebrow. Remains silent. His dark eyes are hypnotic, so I look away.

When I do, I see the two actress-slash-model-wannabes in their brown-on-green Hallowed Grounds aprons, gawking at him and whispering behind the cappuccino machine.

That's just the thing: a guy like Reece? He could have any girl he wanted, anytime.

What would it be like to stroll into a coffee shop and set two voluptuous teenage girls all atwitter? And if you had that power in a town like this, why would you ever, in a million years, make a play for someone like me?

I sigh and when I look back at him, he is smiling.

"You're quite the wordsmith, aren't you?" he asks, his grin dazzling, his cheekbones haunting.

"What does that even *mean*, Reece?" I snap, finishing off my coffee. I'm desperate for another biscotti but just try getting one now with a Greek god sitting across from me and the cashiers drooling.

"It means you don't save your eloquence just for your books. You speak just as articulately in real life. I so hoped you would."

"Hoped I would what? I'm confused. That's the problem. Nothing here adds up. Didn't we just meet? Like last night? Didn't you transfer here from Manhattan because your parents thought a change of scenery would do you good? Stop acting like I'm the reason you're here. It's *not* flattering. Frankly, it's vaguely creepy."

"Creepy or not, you *are* the reason I'm here." He's not smiling. In fact, those chocolate-brown eyes—now a shade darker—are kind of drilling into me, pinning me into my chair, making me want to sit somewhere—anywhere—else.

"How is that even possible? What, because you've read a few of my books? Because you've got a crush on Scarlet Stain and think just because she came out of my twisted teenage brain that somehow I *must* be like her? Here's a news flash, pal: I'm *nothing* like her. OK, maybe I have red hair, but I don't know karate, I don't dress in all black, I don't practice black magic, I've never kicked anyone's butt, and I've definitely never seen a vampire, let alone hunted one, so if that's your twisted little game, then—"

"Oh, but you *are* like her." He leans forward now, that spicy cologne intoxicating, his breath fragrant as it caresses my cheek. "Much more than you know. You have that same savage tongue, and you're not afraid to use it."

"OK," I say, unplugging my laptop and sliding it into my laptop bag. "You're clearly delusional."

"Am I?" He leans in and drops his voice an octave. "I came here for *you*. I haven't just read your books; I've memorized them. They're . . . brilliant. Not in a classic sense, mind you; but as part of the vampire canon, they are nothing short of brilliant."

"What are you, some reporter angling for a story? If so, call my literary agent."

I start to get up, but he stops me with a cold hand on my forearm.

I look desperately around the room, but everyone is either (a) absorbed with their dates or (b) absorbed with themselves—this is Beverly Hills, after all. Suddenly, even the giddy teenybopper clerks who were undressing Reece with their eyes are now fumbling over themselves, frothing up some steamy milk for Eazy Billz, a rapper who's just barged in with his entourage of nine.

"I'm not a reporter," Reece says in a new tone, not a particularly nice one. "I'm not a fan either. I'm a collaborator, a fellow writer, and I have an idea for your next book."

"Wow." I try to snatch back my wrist—and fail. "Now I've heard it all."

He yanks me down from my half-standing position, and I hit the chair hard. It screeches against the rough tile floor, but no one notices, since everyone is murmuring about Eazy and his latest platinum album.

Suddenly, I'm scared.

Beverly Hills or no, I've read enough news stories to know that bad things happen, even to good girls.

Yes, we're in a clean, comfy, well-lit place, but just outside that door, two streets away, is a sketchy alley where anything could happen.

There is no Wyatt to save me, no Abby to tell me to run, no Scarlet Stain to leap through the ceiling tiles and impale this creep on one of her tailor-made daggers, swords, or maces. It's just me and my horrible, no-good, rotten instincts.

With all the commotion in the room, all the stargazing and self-importance, Reece could literally drag me up by my arm, zip me out of the store, whisk me somewhere dark and lonely, and no one, not a soul, would think twice or remember a single detail.

I can just hear the police interrogation now:

*"What, Officer? Nora who? No, I don't know who was sitting there."*

*"She might have had red hair, maybe blonde. Brown?"*

*"Are you sure it was a girl sitting there, 'cause I could have sworn it was a guy!"*

A tremor passes through my body but never gets farther than my forearm, maybe because Reece still has my wrist clamped tight.

"Sit down and listen," he barks above the din. "It's very simple. You have a deadline; I have an idea. You are running out of stories, and I have one that will spark your creativity like a firecracker in a pile of dead leaves. We *will* work together. It's just that simple. Be it now or later, our . . . partnership is inevitable."

I stare back at him, my mind reeling, palms sweaty, heart racing.

*How* does he know I'm on a deadline?

*How* does he know all my ideas have dried up?

What's more, how did he know to find me here tonight?

There are too many questions, too many coincidences, for this to be anything good . . . or natural.

At last I wrench my hand free and stand, though it takes everything I've got—and then some. I storm past saying, "Abby was right. You *are* a stalker."

"Abby should watch her tongue, then, shouldn't she?" He stands, his face inches from mine. His eyes are even darker, his lips thin and gray as he adds, "Or she'll end up like Bianca."

# CHAPTER 6

The TV is glowing and blaring when Abby gets home that night after another late shoot on the *Zombie Diaries* set.

She gives me the universal, big-eyed, openmouthed, hands-in-the-air *What's up?* sign—I almost never watch regular TV, so she *must* be shocked—and I point to the live feed currently spilling across the fifty-five-inch flat-screen in reply.

"Bianca's missing," I say simply, the pit of my stomach empty from half-crying ever since I left Reece at the Hallowed Grounds café.

"Oh my God," she says, sitting next to me on the couch and instinctively reaching for my hand. "When? How?"

"They don't know," I answer, wincing as she touches the bright-red spot where Reece held my wrist just hours earlier. "She was supposed to make a shareholder's meeting at her dad's corporate offices after school, and when she didn't show, her father told the cops. They started digging, calling her teachers at home, even some of her classmates. No one's seen her since homeroom."

"But that's crazy. You're *sure* she wasn't in food and culture class today?"

I shake my head. “She wasn’t in any of our classes today. Not one.”

“Except for homeroom,” she says, voice barely above a whisper. She’s clutching my hand. I wince again, and this time she notices. She takes her hand away, and although I rush to cover the bruise with the sleeve of my white hoodie, she sees it and gasps. “What *is* that? Who *did* that?”

I cover it. “Nothing, Abs. Nobody.”

“Nobody nothing,” she says in her best acting-like-a-concerned-parent voice. “I can see the finger marks from here. You tell me who did that, or I’ll call Wyatt and—”

“No, no, don’t call Wyatt. He already thinks I’m stupid enough as it is. It was . . . Reece, OK? It was Reece, and I don’t care what you think or how wrong it is not to say anything. I just don’t want anyone to know. OK?”

“Reece did that?” she stands up, pacing between the cluttered coffee table and the TV. “When? How? *Why*? Why would a guy you’ve only just met do something as . . . violent as that?”

“I was down at the Hallowed Grounds after school, trying to get some writing done, and he just . . . showed up.”

“I told you that dude was a stalker,” she says triumphantly, looking at the half-empty box of chocolates on the edge of the coffee table. With one swipe, she slides it off the table and into the wastebasket.

“He was all crazy. Apologizing for flaking out on me today at school one minute, then threatening me the next.”

“Threatening you how?” The TV grabs Abby’s attention, blasting Bianca’s yearbook picture on the local news.

It’s the photo from last year, the same one they’ve been running on every station now since I returned from the café, barred the door, and started flipping channels just to get Reece's angry, accusatory voice out of my head. "Nothing, really. He just . . . He says he has this idea for a book, a Better off Bled book, and that we're going to write it together . . . or else."

"Or else what?"

I look past her bouncing knee to the TV screen, which still shows a close-up of the quite gorgeous, quite missing Bianca Ridley.

"Or else . . . he said . . . I'd wind up like *her*."

# CHAPTER 7

Abby and I are clustered with a few other kids in homeroom the next morning, figuring out the wording for a Missing poster we want to post around the school halls, when none other than Bianca Ridley walks through the door and takes her old seat, like nothing ever happened.

Nobody says anything. Nobody can.

We're all . . . well, *shocked* would be an understatement.

A kind of awkward silence fills the room until Bianca just starts chatting with her posse, whispering and snapping gum and twisting her hair like six kids aren't sitting in front of her with a notepad full of words like *missing* and *foul play* and *parents* and *very concerned.*

Finally Mrs. Armbruster stands up, lowers her knuckles to the top of her desk like a drill sergeant about to drum out a new cadet, juts her jowly but lovable face forward, and says, "Bianca Ridley, you had us all in a state. Do you know everyone in Beverly Hills is out looking for you right now? What do you have to say for yourself?"

And Bianca, still snapping her gum, twisting her hair, looks at us all and says, "Um . . . that it's nice to be loved?"

Mrs. Armbruster wrinkles her nose, adjusts her bifocals, opens her mouth to say more, and then, nonplussed, just sits back down.

That's that.

I mean, what do you say, really?

*Go to the principal's office*?

*You've got detention, missy*?

*Write "I will not pretend to be missing and freak everyone out including people who don't even like me" on the board five hundred times*?

I turn around, look her up and down, and say, "Bianca, what *happened* to you? We all thought you were . . . dead."

"What for?" she says, and suddenly I notice she's not quite as perfect as the day before.

Her hair's a little unkempt, her lipstick's mussed, her shirt's buttoned wrong, and her super-short skirt is super crooked.

"Can't a girl take a mental-health day without some goody-goody putting out an APB?" She sneers at me, Abby, and the class in general.

"Yeah, well, warn somebody next time you want to fall off the planet," Abby says.

"Don't blame *me*." She looks over our heads and at the door. "Blame him."

We turn to find Reece standing in the doorway, wearing a black distressed jacket with the off-white stripes down the sleeves, his jeans tight, his boots untied, his white T-shirt straining against an Olympian's chest. He breezes in our direction, walks right past Abby and me, sits next to Bianca, and . . . plants one square on her lips.

Right there, in front of the whole class, Mrs. Armbruster

included. OK, she's already sleeping again, but still. What if she weren't?

"Ew." Abby groans, turning around.

I wish I could do the same, but I'm transfixed.

A writer word, I know, but the only one that works in such an extreme situation.

I literally can't take my eyes off them.

And I'm far from a voyeur. I mean, gross, but . . . this is more than sexual.

This is, like, behavioral.

It's like watching two gorillas in a zoo and trying to figure out what separates them from Homo sapiens.

"What are *you* looking at?" Bianca asks once they've finally come up for air. She's lining her lips with a fresh coat of gloss from her (real) diamond-studded compact.

"Are you two insane?" I say. "I mean, clinically? As in rubber-room-for-two-bound? Have you lost your frickin' minds? You don't just go missing one day and come back the next and start dating and expect everything to be fine. It's . . . it's . . . *antisocial*."

Bianca looks at Reece, and Reece looks at Bianca, and they have quite a laugh over that one.

"Hey, look," Bianca says, acting bored, "I explained it to my parents, my parents called the cops, I got a stern talking-to by Principal Chalmers on the way into school today, all's right with the world. If they've forgiven me, then what's the big deal? So turn around and face the front if you know what's good for you."

Reece pats her hand. "Now, now, Bianca, don't snap at Nora. It's not *her* fault sour grapes taste so bitter."

"Sour grapes!" I say, soliciting a *harrumph* out of Mrs. Armbruster, but I don't turn around to acknowledge it. I just lower my voice a smidge and ask, "Who would want to go out with a schizophrenic, moody stalker *creep* like him in the first place, Bianca?"

"Hmm, judging from the veins sticking out in your neck, you would!"

And they laugh and laugh, Bianca and Reece and her pretty little minions, taking up the whole back row of homeroom like this is some comedy club downtown and I'm the last-minute amateur about to get yanked offstage by a giant hook lurking in the wings.

Finally I turn, but not before Reece reaches out a cold hand, patting my soft, warm shoulder, and says quietly, just so I can hear, "Ignore me if you must, but know this much: this isn't over."

# CHAPTER 8

Bianca deteriorates throughout the day.

It's nothing major you can point at, like a word written on her forehead or a brand on her wrist or a tattoo on her ankle, but gradually, she just generally . . . morphs . . . into something other than Bianca.

It's kind of like watching an ice sculpture melt.

If you sit there and watch minute by minute, you can barely notice the difference, but if you look away and then look back after an hour or two, what was once a lovely, long-necked swan is now kind of just a shapeless hunk of ice sitting in a bowl of water.

She's still Bianca; don't get me wrong. Same witchy ways, same sharp tongue, same radiant beauty, same kicking clothes. She just turns cold and hard and inhuman by degrees as the day unfolds.

In AP English, she digs her nails into the desk all through class. While we're all struggling through the first chapter of *Crime and Punishment*, her book lies there unopened, and she's scritching-scratching at the top of her desk like a starving artist in her studio. She doesn't look up, doesn't wonder if anybody's watching, doesn't fear the teacher catching her, doesn't seem to care who sees her. It's like she's in her own little world and finishing whatever she's started on her desk is the most important thing on the planet.

After class she stands quickly, blows splinters off her palms, and breezes out of class, one knee-high stocking firm just beneath her shapely knee, the other pooled like an old lady's second skin above her fashionably clunky heels.

Bianca is not herself. I mean, this witch freaks and sends one of her minions to the drugstore across the street for replacements if she gets a run in her stocking, let alone if one of her stockings runs down her leg like elephant skin.

But I'll give her the benefit of the doubt. Maybe she's not feeling so well and just doesn't notice—not likely for an evil superpower like Bianca, but possible.

I make sure she's gone, swing by her desk, and read these words scratched precisely into the surface:

*The night approaches; I can't wait.*

OK, well, a few things.

First, *approaches*?

That's, like, poetry for a girl like Bianca.

Next, *I can't wait*?

For what?

Another nonstop night of carnal relations with Reece?

But the worst is that the message is carved deep, practically right through the top of the desk.

It looks like the work of a knife, a really sharp one, only she didn't have a knife or a nail file or even a pen. She just had her fingernails.

I step away from the desk and follow Bianca's crooked skirt and droopy stockings to food and culture class, where she spends the entire period collecting the little white Styrofoam trays from everybody else's pound of ground round, and when she thinks nobody's looking, tipping them up by one corner so that the blood left behind runs straight into her mouth.

Then she licks her lips, almost seductively, to catch every spare drop—of warm hamburger blood, mind you—she might have missed.

Then, instead of cooking her meatloaf like the rest of us, she slides it into the oven, which she never turned on, which I know because I watched. Then she waits until the other students are busy taking theirs out, hot and fresh, and dumps the pan upside down on a plate and eats it all. Raw. Straight from the pan. With her fingers.

I point it out to Abby, who turns just in time to see Bianca set the empty—and cold!—meatloaf tray down and once again lick every ounce of raw meat off those plump lips.

Abby shivers with disgust, but has long since given up being surprised over Bianca's theatrics. "Probably some new all-protein, raw-food diet."

"Abby, not that I'm any expert—we both know that—but aren't raw foods supposed to be like broccoli and carrots and almonds and figs and stuff? I'm pretty sure all those raw-food health nuts are major vegans, right?"

"So maybe she's cramping major and needs some iron. What do I know? Don't be a stalker, OK? You did this with the snowboarder, remember? You drove me all the way to Burbank just so we could see if he was dating someone else, when all along he was just shopping for new snow boots. It wasn't pretty then; it's no prettier now. Remember what I said about living in your head, writer girl? Now's the time to get out—get out while you can!"

And with that she cuts our meat-free-loaf into eighteen perfect little slices, one for each student in the room—except for Bianca, of course.

With an attitude like that, I figure it's best not to tell Abby about the scratched-in sentence from AP English or what I see later in my last class with Bianca: gym. It's nothing that happens in class, so much as what happens after, in the locker room, no less.

After changing clothes, I linger near my locker, which just happens to be three doors down from Bianca's. I take my time, watching as Bianca talks to her minions, regaling them with Reece's French-kissing prowess at the top of her lungs—all for my benefit, I'm sure—when the moment I've been waiting for finally arrives: the patented Bianca Ridley hair toss.

Now, all girls toss their hair; this we know.

It's as natural to us as stopping to ask for directions, taking the croutons off our salads, or stopping dead in our tracks when we see the word *Clearance!* on a big red sign in a store window.

But not a single girl on this planet, and I'm talking a town full of models, starlets, legends, hookers, and divas, tosses her hair like the one and only Bianca Ridley. This hair toss starts from the arches of her perfectly shaped, size eight-and-a-half feet, ripples through her shapely calves, up her slender thighs, through her size zero waist, up her graceful spine and swan neck, and out through her delicate hands, which flip the hair up and out in such a way that there is literally hang time—like Michael Jordan on the way to the basket in some vintage highlight reel Wyatt made me watch on YouTube once. Her lustrous blonde hair magically hovers in the air until everyone in the room has seen how long and healthy it is, and then and only then does it drift back to her shoulders like it's being gradually released by a flock of cherubs hovering gently around her ears.

And it's in that hang time, those precious 34.2 seconds (or so it seems), that I see what I've been looking for all day, what I've been suspecting since I saw her drain her eighth Styrofoam tray full of blood in food and culture class: two tiny bruises evenly spaced at the nape of her neck, just in the back, which her lustrous hair would normally cover.

Bianca didn't just come back from a mental-health day.

She came back from the dead.

# CHAPTER 9

I want Abby to be there when I test my theory, but she has an early call on the set of *Zombie Diaries 4* and can't hang after school.

I text Wyatt, asking him to meet me by my locker after the final bell, but he's got a callback for a photo shoot for some Swiss watch line that he says would be "great for his portfolio" (whatever *that* is) and can't make it either. (Hmm, maybe if I want more attention, I should seek less-famous friends.)

That's OK. It's a simple test, really, and I can do it from afar, so there's no way I should be in any danger.

Right?

To make sure I'm set up early, I get a pass for the last ten minutes of class from Mr. Simmons, my seventh-period physics teacher, and set up at my locker.

All I have to do is open the door. Everything I need to prove Bianca Ridley is a vampire (I can't believe I'm writing that) is right inside my locker.

The irony of what I'm about to do strikes me as I'm waiting for the final bell of the day to ring. How many times have

I written this scene in a Better off Bled book? How many times has Scarlet Stain had to prove someone is a living vampire before shoving a stake in his heart or loosing a town full of torch-and-pitchfork-bearing peasants on him?

And here I am, standing in the most posh prep school anywhere, in the middle of the day, getting ready to do the very same thing.

The final bell of the day rings loud and clear, the commons area floods with kids—big kids, little kids, rich kids, richer kids, pretty kids, prettier kids . . . and no Bianca.

Now, this girl is always first to her locker after school lets out, hands down.

It's like a contest with her or something.

Last year my seventh-period class was literally right around the corner from my locker—I'm talking six short steps, I counted them one day—and she *still* managed to beat me every single time.

I don't know if she just gets out of her chair and leaves her last class a few minutes early without telling anyone (not that I'd put it past her) or if she's a speed walker or has supersonic shoes or has mastered time travel, but no one gets to her locker faster than Bianca Ridley.

Until this very day.

The one day I'm counting on her to get to her locker faster.

Her locker is only six down from mine, facing my still-open locker door, and she *never* misses an opportunity to freshen her lip gloss, apply some fresh mascara, or study her face . . . until *today*?

Has she pulled another disappearing act?

Is she seducing Reece in the supply closet as we speak?

Is this some master plot to humiliate me in front of the

whole school?

As quickly as the commons area fills with noisy, spoiled, well-dressed brats, it bleeds itself dry, kids running, shouting, skipping toward the bike racks, the bus loop, or the student parking lot as fast as their designer shoes will carry them.

They leave only balled-up wads of paper, empty soda cans, a stray #2 pencil, and dead, dusty silence.

Soon I'm standing there, all alone, my locker still open, my gaze darting left and right, when suddenly I hear their footsteps behind me. One after the other, squeaky shoes on an empty floor. Fast at first, coming faster, then slowing a few yards behind me.

I can't turn too soon or I'll spook her, and she'll wonder why I'm standing there, all alone, my locker open, long after everyone's gone.

But I have to look back in case—well, in case she's turned into some kind of bat or winged monster, fangs drooling mere inches from my neck.

I whip around, just as a hand touches my shoulder—

"Wyatt!" I shout, my heart literally leaping into my throat.

"Yeah, jeez, who'd you expect?"

"Oh my God." I gasp, clinging to his chest as if it's a life raft and I'm leaping off the *Titanic*. "I can't believe it's really you. I thought . . . I thought . . . What are you *doing* here? I thought you had a photo shoot and were too busy to meet me."

He shrugs. "They canceled on me before I could even turn the key in the ignition," he says, sporting a new track-suit—this one all black. "I remembered your text and figured I'd still find you hanging out by your locker. What gives?"

Just then I hear footsteps: *different* footsteps.

Not squeaking but clacking.

Purposeful.

I'd know that witchy walk anywhere. Finally, Bianca is on her way.

I panic. There's no reason for me to be here, alone, after school.

But I'm not alone; Wyatt's here.

Still, there's no reason for me to be here, alone with Wyatt, this long after the final bell unless . . . unless . . .

"Do you trust me?" I ask in a whisper, heart still pounding. I peer up into his deep-blue eyes, already imagining.

He smiles in reply. "What do *you* think, Nora?"

I cut a glance at Bianca, and she is bearing down on us, just rolling out of D-wing and on her way to her locker, her head down, smiling as she writes some wickedly sexy text (probably) to Reece (most likely).

Before she can look up and spot us, I lean in on my tippy toes, grab Wyatt's neck, and pull his warm lips to mine—

Now I know why they say it's like fireworks, this whole kissing thing.

But no, that's not entirely true; kissing Wyatt for the first time is like biting into a firecracker and holding on even though you know it's going to explode and quite possibly rip your whole world open.

It's instant sensory overload, my heart and mind short-circuiting as a jolt of pure desire connects with parts unknown.

*Stay focused, Nora,* I think desperately, even as my fingers probe the back of his head to feel the stubble that was once his dark, flowing locks.

Somehow, I do. Stay focused, that is.

Even above the blood pumping through my ears, I can hear Bianca's heels clattering on the marble floor of the commons area.

Amid the swirl of passion that floods from my toes to my thighs to my heart to my throat, I can sense the vampire's presence, lurking just in the distance.

And then, sweet bliss; Wyatt's lips are soft and gentle. Just like I've imagined every night since I've met him. They are moist too and taste vaguely of some kind of coconut lip balm. (Coconut, really? Could he be wearing it for me? Did he put it on in the car when he read my text?)

I can feel a little resistance, at first, as he gasps, quite sincerely, "Nora," his voice hoarse and gentle. I hold him close, press against him, press hard, and the resistance crumbles like a tissue in a hurricane. We meld together. Even as tall and tough as he is, our bodies gently merge until we share the same tiny space in front of my locker.

His large, warm hands wrap expertly around the small of my back, as if he's touched it a thousand times before, pulling me up and closer to him with ease.

Meanwhile a deep, contented sigh escapes his lips, and just as I'm threatening to go over the cliff, give in to the passion and the heat pounding from his body, my eyes flicker open, I pivot just so, and see Bianca rolling her eyes at us as she quickly dials in the combination to her locker and opens it.

I have only seconds now, but I need to wait until she shuts her locker door to get the full effect.

I sigh, pushing slightly against Wyatt, but not too much.

He doesn't sigh so much as grunt, an animal hunger filling him, filling me as I grunt back in reply.

How many times have I imagined kissing Wyatt this way? Always in fantasies deep inside my head: shoving him into some random locker, ravishing him in the waning afternoon light of another boring school day as dust bunnies from four hundred lockers swirl around us.

And here I am, using Wyatt to spy on Bianca, lying with my lips, telling the truth with my hips, and somewhere, far outside me, in the real world that still exists outside our own personal coconut-flavored heaven, I hear the slam of a locker and am jerked back to reality.

Seconds now, only seconds left. I roughly shove Wyatt away, whip open my locker, and stare straight at the eight-by-ten-inch mirror I have wedged in there.

Beyond Bianca's locker I can see clearly to the double back doors, leading outside to the track and field. My line of vision is clear; there is nothing blocking it. Though there should be. Bianca should be blocking it, blocking everything. There is no Bianca.

I turn all the way around, just to make sure she's still standing there. There she is, plain as day, right where she was, slowly picking lint off her busty sweater as she adjusts her purse strap before leaving.

"Nora, what the—?" Wyatt gasps.

Again I grab his neck, this time shoving his face toward the mirror. "Look, Wyatt. *Look.*"

He does, he sees, he looks behind him, eyes wide, looks back in the mirror at where Bianca should be and . . . nothing. Just an empty row of lockers backlit by the double doors to the track.

It's like one of those illusions you see in magic shows, where the magician uses a special mirror to make his pretty assistant disappear.

Only, in our case, this isn't magic. Or maybe it is.

*Black* magic.

"Oh my God." He looks me deep in the eyes. "How did you know?"

I take one of my complimentary copies of Better off Bled #4 from the top shelf of my locker (I always like to keep a few handy, you know, for the freshmen), shove it into the middle of his chest, and snap, "Are you kidding me? This is what I do!"

By the time he's grabbing my arm and pulling me out to the student parking lot, Bianca is gone, but the commons aren't entirely empty.

Standing in a corner, hidden from even Bianca herself, I see a very familiar shape. Looming, dark.

Just after Wyatt enters the hallway leading from the commons, and just before I follow him, the shape emerges from the shadows and smiles.

Reece is watching; Reece *was* watching.

And now he knows that we know.

I think he's smiling, but I'm wrong. It's just his fangs poking out from his upper jaw, puffing his lips out, curling them upward.

It only looks like a smile.

His dead, dark eyes say something completely different.

And it's not good.

For either of us.

# CHAPTER 10

"So tell me this," Wyatt says after his fourth chocolate-covered biscotti at Hallowed Grounds an hour later. "Was there anything *not* manipulative about you kissing me just so Bianca wouldn't suspect you were trying to catch her in the act of being a . . . a . . . whatever she is?" He leans in close so as not to be overheard, his eyes alive and bright, his throat still flush. Whether that's from my kiss or Bianca's vampire status remains to be seen.

"Yes, I mean, no, I mean . . . It's complicated, Wyatt, OK?" I say, looking over his shoulder to the front door, half expecting Bianca and Reece to storm in—maybe even fly in—any minute.

"Do you have somewhere to go?" he says, reaching for his second hot chocolate. "I think, considering the fact you tricked me into meeting you after school today, lured me into a false kiss, and used me like a piece of meat, you at least owe me a thoughtful and careful explanation."

I laugh for the first time since, well, since Bianca disappeared. No, no, earlier than that: since Reece appeared.

"You're right, of course. So let me be brutally honest here because this day is a game changer. Wouldn't you agree?"

"Game changer? It's a life changer! An, an . . . *afterlife* changer." His voice is low. The café is crowded this time of day, and even as insensitive a lout as he can be, Wyatt knows this is deadly serious business.

I mean, it's not every day you find out the hottest chick in school is actually a desk-scratching, raw-hamburger-eating, no-reflection-giving-off, bloodsucking vampire!

"I mean, there's no use in hiding it anymore. I like you, Wyatt, a lot. Have I imagined kissing you in the heat of passion before? Sure, OK, yeah. Only about five *bazillion* times! Was today one of them? No, not really. Did I use you? Absolutely, but seriously . . . do you care?"

He smiles, blushes, avoids my gaze, and reaches for another sip of hot chocolate, but a quick peek tells me the cup's empty. "No," he finally admits, a little sheepishly. "I mean, if that's what getting used feels like, well, use me whenever you want." He fiddles with the to-go lid on his brown-and-green, eco-friendly Hallowed Grounds cup and asks, "So, you feel like using me anymore today? Like . . . right now . . . for instance?"

I look at his arms, golden brown in the late-afternoon sunlight, his one-size-smaller-than-it-probably-should-be gray T-shirt hugging every one of his masculine curves.

Suddenly I ask, "Well, I mean, did you feel *anything*?"

"When?" he asks, playing dumb. "Where?"

"Back there, doofus, when I . . . I . . . attacked you."

He leans forward, looking around before pinning me with those deep-blue eyes. "Of course I did. You think I stop by your dorm suite night after night hoping to get another look at Abby in her stupid zombie makeup or to grab a free cola? I can afford my own cola. I don't even really like cola. Of *course* I feel something for you. It's just, I dunno, you seem like you'd rather just be . . . friends."

"I do, kind of," I confess, although it kills me to say it.

He leans back, a pout pulling down those beautiful puffy lips and instantly making me regret my words.

"What I mean is," I blather, "I'd rather be friends than get my heart broken again. Look at you. Are you going to sit there and tell me you're ready to have a serious, committed relationship when every other day you're snapping pictures next to some half-naked supermodel? How can I compete with that?"

"By giving me a sign. Any sign," he says, leaning even closer. His breath smells vaguely of gourmet hot chocolate and mini marshmallows.

"Well, I would consider making out with you in the commons for nearly three minutes a pretty big sign that I'm into you, *OK*? If you can't pick up on that big of a sign, well, I'm not sure what else to do."

He smiles like a kid at Christmas and then reaches out across the table and holds my hand gently, like an old-school boyfriend.

No one has ever done that, ever, in all my life.

And it feels so funny, his gaze on mine, so familiar and suddenly so . . . different.

Is that what it was like for him and Abby when they crossed the threshold from friend to boyfriend and girlfriend for those two months last year?

Did he see her differently?

And she him?

I can still taste his coconut lip balm on my tongue, and

the urge to taste it again is almost too strong to resist.

"So . . . now what?" He scratches the back of his head with his free hand.

"Now? Well, now I suppose we tell Abby and hope we don't hurt her feelings when she sees us together and—"

He squeezes my hand gently and says, "OK, yeah, that too but more importantly what are we going to do about Bianca being a . . . you know?"

"Oh." I blush, instantly feeling fifty shades of stupid. "Well, there's not much we can do. I mean, the cops won't believe us. Principal Chalmers already bought her little song and dance about needing a mental-health day. I suppose we just have to keep an eye on her—and each other—until she makes some kind of a—"

Just then his phone skitters across the table, ending up in a pile of empty biscotti wrappers before he can pick it up and read the incoming text.

"Oh," he says, getting up quickly and letting my hand go like a wet eel, "the shoot is back on. I need to be there in fifteen, and it's halfway across town."

His satchel and jacket are on the back of his chair. He grabs them both and looks down. "Come with me," he offers, his long fingers reaching for mine. "That way I know you'll be safe."

"I'm fine," I say a little defensively, ticked off that he could leave me so easily, especially considering what we've both just seen. "I'm here. It's the middle of the day. What can happen?"

"I just don't know how long the shoot will take, and I don't want you being alone."

"That's sweet, but . . . I can take care of myself."

He frowns. "Isn't that what Scarlet Stain always says . . . just before Count Victus traps her in some dastardly scheme and she secretly wishes she hadn't acted so brave and let her brand-new boyfriend run off to a photo shoot without her?"

I snort, relieved he can read me so well but still wishing he wouldn't put his work over me. What, like he's going to change his mind and give up a chance to make a few quick grand with one of fashion's hottest photographers just to sit around some coffee shop with nerdy old me?

"How's this?" I ask, shooing him off. "I'll leave before dark, rush back to the dorm, lock the door, and stay put until you come to save me, OK?"

"Be more specific," he warns, slipping the jacket over his perfect chest and the satchel over his perfect shoulder. "Text me the minute you're leaving here and the minute you get inside the door of your dorm. If it takes longer than ten minutes, I'll be there, no matter what."

I smile, thinking that was sweet, and watch his tight little rump exit the building—me and every other chick in the café, not to mention those two guys by the window. This shoot—and every shoot—is too important to cancel on account of some hysterical girlfriend.

Or BFF.

Or casual make-out groper in the halls.

Or whatever it is he thinks—or I think—I am.

# CHAPTER 11

Reece catches me in the lobby, next to the chest of drawers by the staircase, the one with the chipped porcelain knobs and scratched claw feet.

It's 7:18 p.m., the sun has just set, and it takes exactly twenty-two seconds from the time I walk into the lobby to check my mail and get shoved into the stairwell nobody uses. Ever.

He has no rope, no gun, no knife, no dagger, no handcuffs, no chains. He has only his bare hands and his inhuman strength.

Suddenly I am pinned to the wall, arms at my side, Reece's face inches from my own, fangs trembling. "Hello, Nora," he seethes, his fangs making his voice sound different, slightly feminine but no less spooky. "Enjoy your . . . *date*?"

"I sure did," I somehow manage, straining my wrists against his cold, deadly grip. "How about you?"

He smirks, stepping back slightly, releasing me. "Oh, that Bianca. She's quite the catch."

"I bet." I rub my wrists in front of my chest, looking at the door.

"Try it, and I'll snap your neck in six places by the time you take your second step."

"Why?" I shout, hoping someone—anyone—will hear me. "Why me? Why are you *doing* this to me?" I hate the frantic tone in my voice, but what can I say? This kind of thing doesn't happen to me every day.

"I told you why. And lower your voice. You've delayed my plans long enough. I won't have you stall anymore by siccing your neighbors on me."

"Why are you doing this?" I say, quieter this time, deliberately biting off each word to ensure I finally get an answer to my question.

"I already told you. I need your special skills. I need you, I need you now, and you will not deny me again."

"What are you going to do? If I refuse, I mean? Are you going to turn me into a vampire, like you did Bianca?"

He looks vaguely surprised I'd make the suggestion.

"Of course not. You would be useless to me then."

I smile, suddenly holding all the cards.

"Well, if you need me, and you can't turn me, then what's the big deal? Why should I care? You can't hurt me, so what power do you hold over me?"

Now he smiles. "You're right. I can't hurt *you*, per se, but I can hurt what's important to you. Or should I say, *who*'s important to you."

"Don't you dare," I shout, pounding on his marble-hard chest with my soft, useless hands. "Don't you dare *touch* them."

"Then do what I want." He pushes me back against the wall, his face in mine now. We're so close, I can see the tips of his fangs are not as perfectly white as the rest of his teeth but instead are weathered and worn. "Do what I want, and nobody gets hurt. Hmm, I've always wanted to say that! It's so easy, Nora, to do what I require. So simple, for someone of your . . . talents. Why do you resist?"

"Because," I say, inching for the door, surprised when he lets me get all the way there, put my hand on the knob, and open it without, as he'd promised, snapping my neck in six places, "I write *about* vampires, not *with* them."

And with that I'm gone, out the door, around the corner to the elevator, through the doors, pushing the button, up to the sixth floor, and in sixteen steps I'm behind my own door, bolted shut, every light on, the biggest knife in the kitchen drawer resting in my hand as I sit in the love seat, facing the door.

And still his laughter echoes in my ears, as loud and as close as if he were in the room with me.

# CHAPTER 12

I'm still right there, knife still in hand, head on my chest, when Abby gets home just past midnight. The slamming door wakes me, and I snap up.

Abby stands there, her eyes wide. "Hey, Nora, what's with the big-ass knife?"

I don't answer her. Instead I ask, "Has Wyatt texted you lately?"

She drops her script, keys, and greasy bag of goodness from the local vegetarian drive-through on the coffee table, then drags her pink phone from her jacket pocket. Scrolling through, she frowns and wrinkles her nose. "No."

"Me neither." I nudge my phone, where it rests on the coffee table, with my foot. "Don't you think that's odd?"

She shrugs, which I know from experience is one step away from an eye roll.

"Not if he got lucky working out at the gym or pumping gas or buying gum at the drugstore. You know that guy. All he has to do is step out the door, and chicks are all over him. Why do you think we finally broke up? It was like dating Bra—"

"No, this is different, Abs," I say, interrupting her as much to quit hearing about other girls as to tell her what I need to say. "We, we . . . saw . . . something today, after school, after you left."

"We, whom? You mean . . . you and *Wyatt*?"

Abby is no dope, and joke as she might about her and Wyatt breaking up, it's still a sore spot for her. Because, just like me and my fabled snowboarder, it wasn't quite as mutual as she'd have me believe. And all this time, though I'd never admit it to her, the reason I never tried harder to be with Wyatt was out of loyalty to her. All may be fair in love and war, but roomies have a code, right?

Now her eyes are alive, almost fiery, and I resist the temptation to correct her with a curt "We, *who*?"

"Yeah, my point is, he knew I was upset," I say. "He knew he left me hanging and . . . and . . . after what happened, he would have called. I just know it."

"After *what* happened? What *happened*?" And she is angry. Angrier than I thought she would be.

I'd sat there for hours, clutching my knife, waiting for Reece to appear out of the mist and fly at my throat to finish the job.

Waiting for Bianca to break down the door and gouge out my eyes with those desk-writing claws of hers.

Waiting for them both to tag team me with vampire wrestling moves until I was in pieces on the dorm suite floor.

When they didn't, I let my mind stray to Wyatt, to his kiss, his warm, soft lips, his rough but tender hands, the way he'd expertly pulled me to him, the way his large hands felt on the small of my back, the swell of heat beneath his shiny track pants . . . and how I would tell Abby.

When I would tell Abby.

What I would say, what tone I would use, how loud or how soft, where I'd be standing when I said it, and how long I'd wait after she got home.

I'd even said a few lines out loud, you know, the way they do in cheesy movies—or vampire books:

"It just happened, Abby." (Followed by my sad face.)

"We didn't mean to hurt you, Abby." (Said with a hand on her shoulder.)

"You're not mad, are you, Abs?" (Said in an indignant tone.)

And always, in my imagination anyway, she was kind and understanding and gentle.

The Abby who took being a B-movie star in stride, who signed autographs for hours after dinner on the rare nights she had off from her busy shooting schedule, who'd gladly loan me the most expensive outfit in her closet for a book signing and not care a whit if I brought it back with Sharpie stains all over the sleeves.

I never considered this Abby: the jealous Abby, the still-in-love-with-Wyatt Abby.

Suddenly her eyes are alive and suspicious—and she's waiting for an answer.

And I know if I don't give her one—right now—that will *be* her answer. She'll know immediately what she already clearly suspects.

In a split second, I blurt out my confession. "We didn't see Bianca's reflection in my locker mirror today after school!"

I wasn't going to tell Abby.

Not this, anyway.

I wasn't going to tell her about Bianca—about our proof.

She hadn't believed me in food and culture class, and I

figured one revelation was enough for the night. But in my exhaustion, my fear, my shame, I confessed to something unbelievable over something . . . wonderful.

"Oh, this again?" she says casually, reaching for the white bag with the red-and-green Veggie Heaven logo on the side. "Seriously, give it up. So she dissed you in front of Reece. Big whoop. It's happened a million times before; it'll happen—"

"It's more than that," I say even as she divvies up our standing midnight-after-work order: two small bags of broccoli bites and spinach puffs for each of us. "It's real this time, and it's not just me. Wyatt saw it too."

I sink my teeth into a broccoli bite. It's so good, so hot and real, that it reminds me I haven't had anything to eat or drink since half a biscotti—Wyatt stole the rest—at Hallowed Grounds.

That was hours ago. Long, lonely, scared, anxious hours.

Abby finishes off her spinach puffs and starts in on the broccoli bites, saying around a mouthful of both, "Now you're involving *him* in your paranoia?"

"Well, yeah, I didn't mean to, but . . . I was scared."

"OK, I get that. So what do you think you saw that has you sitting up with a pathetic butcher knife in your hands at 12:30 in the morning? Just like, I might add, a character in one of your books."

"Bianca had no reflection, Abby. She wasn't there. I mean, she was standing right there, and we could see her with our eyes, but when we looked in the mirror, she wasn't there."

"There . . . where? When?"

"After school today! Wyatt and I were hanging out by my locker waiting. I have that big mirror in my locker, you know, and when Bianca showed up, we both looked—no reflection.

She was there, right behind me. I should have been able to see her and, poof, nothing was there. I didn't want to rely on my own eyes, so I asked Wyatt to look. He saw it too. It was like we could see right through her, to the lockers behind her, the doors, the track field beyond, but only in the mirror."

"What is this?" she asks with that here-she-goes-again tone, getting up and tossing our empty fast-food wrappers into the trash before grabbing two Jolt Colas from the fridge. "Another scene from one of your books? You're trying out some new material on me? Or should I say *old* material, because I don't mean to rain on your picnic, but that's like really bad movie stuff. And I should know, girl. I'm the queen of bad movies. Even the writers for *Zombie Diaries* wouldn't touch that old shtick with a ten-foot pole. Not being able to see a vampire in a mirror. Nora, you of all people should know better."

She harrumphs back into her seat and slides me a cold Jolt, old-time saloon-style, the glistening red-and-yellow can skidding down the entire length of the coffee table as if it were wearing roller skates.

I pick it up and suck at it greedily, suddenly thirsty, the triple caffeine rocketing through my veins like a freight train—on speed and acid—heading straight for my already frazzled brain.

"Abby, please listen to me. I know how stupid this sounds; trust me. I know how much it sounds like something out of some stupid vampire book. There's no other way to say the impossible without it sounding impossible. But you *have* to believe me. I'm not making this up. It's not some vendetta against stupid Bianca, whom I couldn't care less about, whatever you and Wyatt think. It's not even about Reece. This is about vampires, real vampires, in our school. It's about our safety. It's about life and death."

I tell her the rest as we finish our sodas: about Reece in the shadow of Bianca's locker, his fangs, his threats in the lobby stairwell. I show her the fresh bruises on both of my biceps from where he held me tight against the rough concrete wall. I tell her that's why I was sitting there with a knife when she came in.

I can tell she doesn't believe me, thinks I'm being hysterical. But whether she's concerned about vampires or about my sanity, either way she's on red alert.

Fueled with enough green veggies to make Popeye proud and enough caffeine to fuel a shuttle to the moon and back, we pledge to stay up all night and keep a constant vigil on the front door.

We *almost* make it.

# CHAPTER 13

Wyatt *is* missing.

Abby and I race to homeroom the next morning, late because we both stayed up so late waiting for him, late because Abby's alarm clock was covered by six pillows and a goose-down-filled duvet, late because she had to stop for coffee on the way. His seat is empty by the time we burst into Mrs. Armbruster's room a full six minutes after third bell.

No, that's not entirely correct. His seat isn't empty, because Reece is using it as a footstool.

"Get off!" I shout, slapping his feet away before I sit down.

"Testy," he says, looking refreshed and at peace as he keeps his size-twelve boots right where they were.

Bianca is at his side, dutiful but not looking quite so hot.

Whatever deterioration she started yesterday is still going on today, only . . . double-time.

Her hair is limp, the roots dirty and brown in the center of her scalp.

Her skin is pale, bordering on gray, her eyes dark where they were once green, yellow where they were once white.

She covers them quickly with big Gucci sunglasses when she sees me studying her, but it's too late. Her hand is shaking, and I see moisture on her palms and armpits.

I think back to the vampire lore I studied to write Better off Bled #2, which features a pivotal scene in which Scarlet is forced, chained to the wall, by Count Victus to watch a friend of hers *turn*, the vampire term for becoming one of them. I described then the same symptoms I'm seeing now: limp hair, dull eyes, excessive sweating, shallow breath, a change in eye color, pale skin as the human body is literally transformed into the living dead.

According to my research, it is supposed to take seventy-two hours, meaning Bianca is already halfway there, presuming Reece turned her the day she went missing.

I almost feel pity for her, what she must be going through, the changes in her body—the pain and discomfort—as her dead cells are overtaken by silent predators, blood-hungry cells taking over and changing everything, inside and out.

Then I imagine how much stronger, more vicious and evil she'll be tomorrow, and the image quickly fades.

I take my seat, breathing heavily, sliding forward to distance myself from Reece and Bianca.

I'm not alone. Even Bianca's once-faithful girlfriends—*minions*, I call them, while Abby prefers the term *posse*—have distanced themselves, taking seats on the other side of the room.

It's as if they think whatever she has might be catching.

So now it's just the happy couple, feet up on Wyatt's chair, as Mrs. Armbruster clears her throat. "Nora," she says, imperiously, as she does everything. "Might I have a word up at my desk, please?"

Abby looks at me questioningly before I get out of my seat and trudge to the teacher's big, oak desk, acutely aware that

I haven't bathed in twenty-four hours and barely had time to brush my teeth, let alone match my socks, before rushing out of the dorm that morning.

"Nora," Mrs. Armbruster whispers, a concerned look on her face as her bifocals rest on her large, pendulous breasts, "have you seen Wyatt this morning?"

I shake my head, afraid if I speak, my voice will crack and give Reece that much more ammunition.

"Well"—Mrs. Armbruster sighs, her sad, hazel eyes looking tired and wan—"I'm very concerned. He's such a sweet boy, and I know he has many demands on his time—you all do, and don't I know it—but he always gets to homeroom on time. And you, too, and Abby. And now you're rushing in late, looking like something the cat dragged in, barking orders at that horrible Bianca and that dramatic new student, Reece.

"Is everything quite all right? I know it can be stressful, all these grown-up demands on you, your talent, your time—and you're still just children, the way I see it. We have excellent counselors here, if you're . . . troubled. Or if Wyatt is, or if you're troubled *because* Wyatt is."

I smile, looking into her eyes surrounded by deep laugh lines and lit by kindness.

Is she ready to hear that vampires really exist?

That they go to her school?

That they sit in the back of her classroom?

"No, it's just typical teenage drama, Mrs. Armbruster. Promise. We'll straighten it out on our own time, and we won't disrespect you by being late again."

Mrs. Armbruster frowns, shakes her head. "It's not me I'm worried about, dear. Just remember . . . I'm here, whatever you need."

I smile, walk slowly back to my seat, and give her a reassuring wink when I'm finally sitting down, but she's already gently snoozing.

Abby looks over at me and whispers, "What was *that* all about?"

"Nothing," I whisper back. "She just—"

But Abby's phone is vibrating, and I know what that means: another early call, some reshoots on her new movie, a photo shoot, whatever. We all know the drill by now.

Even Mrs. Armbruster recognizes the telltale ringtone from Abby's agent and has an office pass waiting for her by the time my best friend gathers up her big purse and clomps from the class, giving me a rushed smile over her shoulder before the real world takes her away.

Once the door has closed behind her, Mrs. Armbruster is silently dozing again above her roll book. When the scattered clusters of cliques and plotters have gone back to their hushed conversations, Reece leans forward until his lips are mere centimeters from my ear.

My entire body wants to bolt, to scream, but I force myself to sit straight and quietly and not move a muscle, lest he think I'm weak again.

"And then there was one," he says, breath oozing across the nape of my neck, caressing the very spot where he bit Bianca.

"If it's the right one," I say through gritted teeth, "one is all it takes."

And just like that, the bell rings. For once I'm the one with the last word!

I rush from class on shaky legs, clear of the door and deep into the halls before Reece and Bianca can even rise.

# CHAPTER 14

And still, Reece beats me to my locker. How—when I left the room a full minute before he did—is anybody's guess.

He stands in front of it and won't budge, even when kids on either side of him give us dirty looks and whisper not so subtly.

Once they are gone, he asks, "Have you ever skipped school? In all your days at Nightshade Academy, have you ever once just . . . ditched?"

"What do you think?" I ask, clutching my AP English book to my chest.

"I think it's a good time to start." He leads me by the arm through the emptying commons and out toward the student parking lot.

I don't resist. I follow him willingly, eagerly, because of one thing: Wyatt.

He must have him hidden somewhere. It's the only explanation.

He races across the lot, head down, hands in his pockets, the California sun bright and clear across what little of his pale skin remains not covered by his leather jacket, long skinny jeans, thick black boots, dark sunglasses, and backward baseball cap.

I linger as he opens the door to a gleaming silver Mercedes, making him get in first to avoid any more exposure to the harsh light of day.

"I thought your kind avoided the sun at all costs," I murmur as I slide into the leather of the passenger seat and close the heavy door.

"The older you are," he says, pushing a glowing blue button on the dashboard as the engine purrs to life, "the more resistant you are to the UV rays."

"Resistant?" I ask as he cruises from the crowded parking lot of Nightshade Academy and out into the sparse midmorning traffic. "But not immune?"

"Never immune, dear Nora. At least, not while one is still alive."

"Where are you taking me?" I ask as we cruise past Rodeo Drive and into—and then quickly out of—Beverly Hills proper.

It feels odd to be on the road—to be anywhere other than the marble-lined halls of Nightshade Academy—this early in the day.

The sky above is a pristine California blue, little white clouds few and far between.

The air has a hushed feel to it, and not just because we're trapped in this coffin of a car. It's like life is on hold, for everybody, until I get this mess sorted out.

Traffic is still thick with go-getters hustling between lanes, but few are as aggressive as Reece as he steers the silver bullet of a car through the pristine streets.

Huge mansions dot our path, giving way to gleaming

office buildings wedged between old-school mission-style offices with Spanish-style roofs or sleek, modern-looking cafés lined with uncomfortable-looking metal tables for two, few of them bustling at this early hour.

Every building has character, that tragically hip and loaded-with-history silver-screen character, and how I wish I could just step out at the next light and take leave of this claustrophobic car and angry driver.

How I wish I could walk away from the way this story is unfolding and trash this plotline the way I've been trashing so many of Scarlet Stain's lately.

Wouldn't it be nice if there were a trash bin for life, where you could drag all the scary, rotten, evil, mean, wicked moments and delete them permanently?

But even those computer files are never truly gone, I've heard. Instead, they haunt the innards of your computer where they lurk, just out of sight.

No, there is no way to delete or rewrite this particular scene. For once, I'm not the author. Reece is.

"We're going to a place where you'll be spending a lot of time," he says as the neighborhoods we pass through suddenly grow more urban, then industrial, then . . . deserted.

I watch the streets zip past the tinted windows, darker than must be legal, hoping to remember where he's taking me.

"No need to memorize the details," he says impatiently, as if this is amateur hour on some prime-time cop show and he's the crusty veteran policeman to my eager but clueless rookie. "I'm not kidnapping you, after all. You'll be free to come or go as you please. But I promise you that once you hear my offer, you'll find it hard to resist."

Ugh. Nothing worse than a smug-ass vampire.

We ride in silence for another few minutes, the beauty, history, and charm of Beverly Hills long gone as we pass derelict brick factories and junkyards until we come to a large warehouse at the end of an industrial cul-de-sac. It is bordered on one side by an empty field, on the other by a fenced-in lot full of rusty cars.

He pulls around to the back of the warehouse, a long and dusty journey in itself, and as we emerge from the car, I hear nothing but the hum of vehicles flying by on the distant highway and crickets chirping in the vacant lot next door.

"Peaceful, isn't it?" he asks over his shoulder. A gleaming new padlock hangs from a twisting length of rusty chain link around two door handles, and he slides a small key in, his long pale fingers are swift and agile. He pauses abruptly. "So peaceful," he repeats, as if to himself. "No one to hear you scream, Nora. No one to run to if you dared. No one to listen to your story if you found the courage to tell it. This is my kind of place." Then, quickly, he returns to the lock.

The chain falls to the ground, where he leaves it—no need to worry about anyone breaking in or neighbors stumbling across it.

We both step over it to enter the main doorway. Inside, the floor is rough concrete covered by years, maybe decades, of dust, sand, and rat droppings. It is vast and hopeless.

The walls are a drab tan, covered with grime and dust and oil and grease and the odd swatch of indecipherable graffiti, long since faded.

The skeleton of old, rusty machinery sits here and there, with no rhyme or reason, their working parts long ago raided for metals and anything else the squatters who spent time here could pawn, recycle, or perhaps stab each other with.

It goes on forever, longer than it is wide, and endlessly long at that.

Dozens—who knows, maybe hundreds—of broken windowpanes circle the ceiling. They let in dusty, diffused light that takes so long to get to the floor, it's orange and muted by the time it arrives.

The warehouse is at least three or four stories tall, but there are no other floors, save for an office way in the back, roughly the size of my mom's old trailer, accessed by a single, steep metal staircase that's missing about half the rungs in the middle. The office windows are broken, with toilet paper hanging out of one and reaching almost all the way to the floor below. It's the kind of place you could ride a bike around three or four times, front to back, back to front, and be winded.

Here and there random signs of human life appear: a discarded milk crate, a broken beer bottle, a can with the top cut off and full of sand and cigarette butts, a crumpled Nacho Tacos bag.

We stand just inside the doorway for a quiet moment. Our eyes—or perhaps just my eyes—adjust to the dim lighting. He marches forward, no doubt expecting me to follow. Dutifully, without argument, I do. Our careful footsteps echo across the wide expanse, the whole warehouse endless and broken and rusty and gross.

Except . . .

Except for a section there to the left, which has been swept, sanded, smoothed, tiled, and separated by three oriental screens. They are beautiful, luxurious, and I'm immediately drawn to them. I step closer without asking permission, and Reece follows without giving any. They look so out of place in this depressing dungeon.

"What is this place?" I ask, moving steadily toward the red-and-black screens, which are covered with traditional Japanese drawings: sumo wrestlers and petite women in flowing kimonos. Each screen has four panels, and the tops billow in alternating silky white drapes that cascade down to cover the gaps where the screens bend.

"This?" Reece asks, dangerously close to the back of my neck as I approach the opening of the three bordering screens. "This is for you, Nora. This is *all* for you."

I enter the opening of the room (I don't know what else to call it), stepping onto a grand woven black-and-red silk rug that covers the entire floor.

In the middle of the rug is a big black desk, the kind only an author could fully appreciate—a place to spend a lot of time, with plenty of room up top for papers and books and pages and drafts and pens and pencils and sodas and open bags of chips but also plenty of legroom below for fidgeting when the ideas just won't come but the pages are due anyway.

If I had a house of my own, somewhere up in the Hills, with a home office, a great view, lots of windows to let in all that beautiful California sun, and hardwood floors to roll my chair across, it's just the kind of desk I would choose.

On top of the desk is a laptop, but not just any laptop. It's the exact same model and year of the one I use to tap out all the Better off Bled books, down to the ergonomic wrist guard and the sleek metallic skin. Nearby is a wireless printer, just as sleek and making me wonder how he could know the very tech I use and feel so comfortable with.

In the space between each of the ornate oriental screens are towering wrought-iron candelabras in all different sizes, the kind you see in Hollywood movies where they have unlimited budgets and a team of people whose whole job, every day, is simply to light the sets.

In all of the candleholders sit flickering candles—long ones and short ones and tan ones and white ones and ivory ones—that fill the roomy space with the scents of ginger and nutmeg.

Thick satin throw pillows as big as couch cushions in all colors of the rainbow lean against each side of the desk.

I approach it cautiously, my hand coming to rest on one of those expensive, space-age, ergonomically correct chairs: the kind with gears and levers and pulleys and hydraulics that hiss when you finally take a seat.

The laptop is open, the screen black.

I brush my finger gently across the mouse pad and the screen flickers to life, revealing a new document, the screen mostly white except for some big, bold type in the middle of the page.

I recognize it immediately as a title page. This is what it says:

> Better off Bled #5:
> *Scarlet's Symphony of Pain*
>
> by Nora Falcon

"What do you think?" Reece asks from the entrance, standing just to the side and looking at me rather than at the glowing laptop screen. "Catchy, huh?"

I turn toward him, his slim body suddenly seeming to block the opening to my private, if glorified cubicle.

Trying to sound brave and dismissive, I say, "Plenty

catchy. I wish you luck with it. My lawyers might have some issues with the title and the subtitle and the byline, of course, but other than that, you should be OK. I already told you—"

"Before you answer," he interrupts, sliding a remote control out of his jacket pocket, "I want you to see something."

"I don't want to see something." I stay put. "I've seen quite enough."

"No," he says, his voice deep and deadly. "You've never seen anything quite like this." And with that dramatic announcement, he steps to the side while pressing a small red button at the top of the remote.

I look past him and focus on a large cube in the middle of the empty warehouse floor. I don't know how I could have missed it when I first walked in, other than the vibrant oriental screens drawing my attention in the opposite direction.

The cube is covered with shimmering silver curtains. They're so shimmery, so thin, they might even be parachutes for all I know. They're billowing now but not from any breeze. Something in the remote has triggered a switch at the top of the cube, and now the curtains fall down the sides of the cube like a waterfall, pooling in great quivering heaps onto the floor.

It's no square; it's a cage.

Inside the cage, arms chained above his head, feet barely touching the floor, is Wyatt.

# CHAPTER 15

"Take him down," I say, rushing out of the frilly room and across the pitted, dusty floor toward the cage.

Reece follows me slowly, dawdling, stepping on glass and rusty tin and not saying a single word as I take in the scene.

Wyatt is still wearing the black track pants from the other day at Hallowed Grounds. His chest is still covered by the too-snug gray T-shirt, coated with the grime of the warehouse and streaked with sweat, probably some tears, and the slightest trace of blood just under his sagging chin. His dirty head lolls across his chest.

I reach the bars, rattle them, feel their heft, their absolute impenetrability, and shriek, "Wyatt!"

He mumbles, shakes his head, then struggles to lift it.

"Nora?" His eyes are cloudy, his beautiful face as dirty as his smelly shirt. "Nora, get out of here. Run!" But it's not an order, not a shout. It's more like a . . . whimper.

His voice is listless, his arms just hanging there, not moving when he does.

The pits of his shirt are sweat-stained. I try to think how long it's been since I've last seen him: over fifteen hours now. Has he been hanging here the entire time? Chained up while I was arguing with Abby to believe me and feeling sorry for myself in my comfortable dorm suite?

His arms quiver with tension, his wrists are bloody and bruised, his feet not quite flat on the unfinished wood floor of the cage. It looks so awkward, so painful. No wonder his voice is barely above a whisper, his chin wearing a groove in the stretched collar of his T-shirt.

I shush him gently and follow his arms from his sweaty pits to his biceps to his elbow to his forearm to his wrists, which are shackled to the bars of the cage midway up. Then I follow his legs from his slim waist to two more sets of shackles chaining his ankles. They're rusty and as impenetrable as the thick steel bars of his twelve-by-twelve-foot cage.

I hear the vague rustle of Wyatt's deep breaths against his sweaty T-shirt. He looks so different—so small and weak and helpless.

In school he is so strong and vibrant that girls watch him with avarice and guys watch him with jealously—even the ones who are prettier than him, because even their beauty can't match his charm and that gorgeous crooked grin. His beautiful blue eyes are dull now, the grin gone, the biceps flaccid, the long legs dangling, and it's all my fault.

Every minute of his pain, every ounce of energy and beauty Reece has stolen from Wyatt is because of me. All of it.

"Despite the grim circumstances," Reece says, suddenly appearing by my side, "I assure you he's quite comfortable. The drugs ensure he's pain-free. Who knows, after our little . . . collaboration, he may not remember a thing. Probably better that way, for him anyway."

I turn to him, blocking out the sight of Wyatt in my peripheral vision. "What do you want me to do?" There is no fight left in me. There is no deal to be made here, no negotiation to enter into, no fight to be won. This is not a scene in one of my books, a scene I can rewrite and twist to fit my needs—or, for that matter, Wyatt's.

This is real life, and for better or worse, I can do merely what I'm told and hope for the best.

"I only ask that you do for me what you already do for a living, Nora. Write."

"Why? What is all . . . this about?"

"What does it matter?" He grunts impatiently, stepping slightly away from the cage as if I should follow. "Why do you care what I want when it is in your power to give it to me, simply and painlessly? You see your predicament. How can you refuse?"

"Obviously I can't," I say through gritted teeth, taking one step closer to him—and away from my best friend. "You have me at your mercy. Great. Good for you. I give you that much. But I'd still like to know *why* you want me to do this."

"All in good time," he assures me without one trace of sincerity. With his hand on my sagging shoulder, he gently urges me away from Wyatt's cage and ushers me across the dirty floor.

I follow him all the way to the desk, all the way into my seat.

When I look up and peer past the laptop, I see that he's situated my office and Wyatt's cage in perfect view of each other. In fact, you couldn't have arranged them any more ideally unless you'd planned it that way, which he obviously has.

I manage to look at him (without spitting) and smirk.

"Seriously?" I nod toward poor Wyatt.

"For inspiration," he explains.

Indeed.

I clench my jaw, force a smile, look away from Wyatt, and peer into Reece's shark eyes. "What's this great idea for a story you have, anyway?"

He sits on a soft red cushion in a black rattan chair in one corner of the room and crosses his legs. He places his pale hands on the armrests as if he's awaiting a cocktail at some country club and not surrounded by filth and decay.

"It's very simple, you see. For four volumes you've had Scarlet Stain chasing Count Victus. For volume five, I simply want you to reverse the formula."

"You want Count Victus to chase . . . Scarlet Stain?" I ask, already seeing the possibilities.

"I do think your readers would enjoy seeing this turn of events, don't you? The hunter becoming the hunted?"

I nod.

"It has . . . *potential*," I admit somewhat reluctantly, although already my mind is racing with the opening scene. "What else?"

"That's it. That's all I require of you."

"Hold up—that's your big master plan? That's why you moved clear across the country, showed up at my book signing, registered at Nightshade Academy, turned Bianca, and kidnapped Wyatt? Because you're tired of seeing Count Victus in the victim role?"

He cocks his head and smiles, though it doesn't reach all the way to his eyes. "Well," he says, putting his fingertips together under his chin, "not exactly. However, that is the deal."

"Just write that story and you'll let Wyatt go?"

"Of course." He sighs. "What do I want with another male vampire?"

I look across the room, my eyes zeroing in on that bloodstain just beneath Wyatt's collar.

My heart is racing with hope, but I purposefully avoid eye contact and as soberly as possible, like a kid on the playground not believing some other kid is going to trade his pudding cup for a cheese stick, ask, "So you haven't . . . turned him yet?"

"Of course not." He scoffs. "We vampires aren't *so* bad. We can still keep our word. After all, a deal's a deal."

"But the blood," I say, looking from Wyatt to Reece.

"Let's just say your friend gave one heck of a fight."

I shake my head. "And Bianca? If all you wanted was to lure me here, using Wyatt as bait, what do you need Bianca for?"

"Why do you care? I thought you two hated each other anyway."

"She hated me, for whatever reason. I never said I hated her."

"Either way," he says curtly, "I can't be all places at once. You have two best friends, do you not? Since even with *my* vast powers, I can be in only one place at a time. Consider Bianca . . . my second skin."

I rise from the chair, but he pins me with a vicious glare. I sit back down.

"If you do anything to Abby . . ." My voice is full of tremors I can no longer hide. There is some threat there, at least the tone of a threat, but for the life of me, I can't finish.

What?

What will I do?

Call his bluff and risk Wyatt's safety?

"Relax, Nora. She's perfectly safe. She won't even know Bianca is shadowing her. I just have to make sure no one comes to your rescue. Hence, I need an ally. Once I got a good look at Bianca, well, I knew she'd be perfect for the job."

I nod, open the laptop, and prepare to type. The sooner I get this over with, the better.

He smiles, watching me from across the room in anticipation.

"Whoa, whoa, whoa. Are you going to sit there, like that, the entire time?"

"I was planning on it, yes," he says, somewhat surprised at my vehement reaction.

"Oh, no." This is a real deal breaker, even when the deal is life or death. "I know you're holding all the cards here, but I really must insist on you sitting somewhere, anywhere, else. You drooling in the corner over every fresh page is going to get real distracting, real quick."

He sighs, stands, and approaches the desk. "I guess it was too much to ask to watch genius at work," he says sarcastically.

An awkward silence follows, my hands poised over the keyboard, his eyes lingering on my hands poised over the keyboard.

"Anything else?"

"Just this one slight detail," he says, reaching down to open a desk drawer and pulling out a single sheet of paper. He hands it to me.

I take it. It looks like a dictionary page. A really cramped dictionary page.

There are four columns, side by side, filling the length of the page. Each column has fifty numbers—one through fifty in the first column all the way to the right of the page, fifty-one through one hundred next to that, and so on, up to two hundred.

Next to each number is a word, all seemingly unrelated: *lake, elm, solstice, farm, equinox.*

"What's this now?"

"It's very simple." He lurks over my shoulder but, I notice, just out of the line of sight of the open laptop monitor. "Every number stands for a page, every word stands for a word I want you to use on that page."

"What? That's crazy. What for? That's going to get really difficult come, say, word seventy-eight. Where does it go on the page?"

"It's simple, really. For the numbers up through ten, it will be the number of words. So, here, number five, will be the fifth word on the page: *travel*. Do you see? I can see where that goes right now. You could say something like *Scarlet Stain loved to travel*. One, two, three, four, five: very simple. Later, when the numbers get to double digits, the pattern shifts again, so that—here—word thirty-five is *our*, meaning in the third line down on the page, in the fifth word over, you will use *our* in a sentence. Not too terribly difficult, is it?"

"Not too difficult?" I squirm, eyes wide with disbelief. (I knew it seemed too easy!) "Are you serious? Do you know how hard it is to find a particular place for some of the words on this list? Solstice? Equinox? These aren't words I use every day, let alone in a Better off Bled novel! How in the world am I supposed to use a word like *restructuring* in a story a teenage girl is going to relate to? I mean, seriously, this is really going to test the limits of creativity," I finish, whining, knowing I'm whining but powerless to stop.

He moves away and points to the cage in the middle of the empty warehouse. "Like I said, for inspiration."

# CHAPTER 16

Abby is scared, and rightfully so.

We sit in the Hallowed Grounds coffee shop, knees up against the table across from each other, neglected chai teas steaming in front of us, uneaten macadamia biscotti still in their plastic wrappers.

I wanted to do this alone, somewhere private, like the dorm suite, but the risk of Reece or Bianca interrupting us, violently, maybe even permanently, forced me to relocate to the twenty-four-hour coffee shop.

I figured the bright lights, the hissing cappuccino machine, the gossipy teenage cashiers, the other frustrated writers, and the public setting would put us both at ease. I figured wrong.

It's late, and I know Abby is tired, her face still slightly pink from scrubbing off her zombie makeup in her trailer after another long night on the set.

"Well, what can we do, Nora? We have to do something! I mean, this is Wyatt we're talking about. What if he's torturing him right now, for God's sake? How can we sit here discussing it like this when our friend is in danger?"

"You think I don't want to rush over there right now and save him?" I lean in so my voice won't travel quite so far. "But you should see this cage. I don't know about you, but my skills for breaking friends out of three-inch-thick metal bars are a little rusty, you know?"

"This is LA." She leans in just as close. "You can find anything here. Dirty deeds done dirt cheap and all that."

"Look around. This is Beverly Hills. I don't see any safecrackers lurking around at pricey cafés in the middle of the night, you know, and I don't think they advertise in the yellow pages."

"So, what, that's it? We just give up, drink our chai tea, and hope for the best?"

"All we can do is what he wants. It's the easiest way."

"What kind of crazy guy is this dude? He comes all the way here, from Manhattan, to force you to write some stupid vampire book?" She is instantly chagrined at the slip of tongue, but it's OK. Fang fiction isn't for everybody, although a seventeen-year-old who dresses up like a rotting corpse every night of the week has very little room to talk. I mean, at least you have to have half a brain to read my books. You don't even need to be able to read to watch her stupid zombie movies!

"I gotcha, Abby," I say, "but I'm not interested in his reasons anymore. I just want Wyatt out of that cage and back with us."

"I mean, can't we call the cops?" she whines, her face looking less pretty and more desperate by the second. "The feds? Somebody, somewhere? You write about this stuff. I mean, aren't there real vampire hunters out there in the world?"

I snort, glad no one is around at this hour to hear us, save for the lone clerk who's busy jamming out to the music vibrating his earphones while he cleans out the cappuccino machine.

"Abby, until yesterday, I didn't even realize vampires existed. What do I know about vampire hunters? And even if there are any, where do we find them? The task is easy. Write his stupid book, use his stupid words, and he'll set Wyatt free."

"Do you trust him to do that?" she asks, hands in the air.

"Of course not, but what else can we do? I know this much: If I write the book, I can also delete the book. I can destroy the flash drives, dump it in the recycle bin on my laptop, something. Heck, I can make sure the book sucks so no one publishes it. Know what I mean? I'm not entirely at his mercy, but I have to play the game until I figure out some type of plan."

"You would do that?" she asks, as if we've just met. "You would purposely write a bad book just to save Wyatt?"

"What? What kind of a jerk do you think I am? I would write ten dozen bad books, each one worse than the last, to save Wyatt."

She shakes her head, her hands buried in her dark-pink-on-lighter-pink turtleneck sweater, her luxuriant chestnut brown hair swept back in a simple ponytail, all the better to see her deep green eyes. Right now those eyes are scared, almost . . . haunted.

"I dunno," she says, chin on one knee. "I just feel so helpless, sitting here knowing Wyatt's in some cage being guarded by some maniac vampire!"

"I know. I know, but you have to keep it together. You have to be strong, Abby, remember that! I'll write as fast as I can, four thousand, maybe even five thousand words a day if possible."

"But how? When?"

"I've already e-mailed Principal Chalmers and my guidance counselor, explaining my publisher's deadline. They've given me the rest of the week off, plus the weekend. I can do it. I can do it by then, but you have to be my eyes and ears at school. I hate to leave you defenseless, but you'll be alone with Bianca and Reece for those few periods every day. Are you up to it?"

"I want Wyatt freed as much as you do," she says, planting her feet on the floor, defiantly taking her first sip of chai tea—and promptly making a displeased face, no doubt at the old bathwater temperature. "What, you don't think I'm up to it? You think I'll crack or something?"

I shake my head, reaching for my own cup of lukewarm tea. The sweet, spicy liquid revives my lips, my tongue, my throat, my very soul.

"Abby, I trust you completely. I just know how Bianca gets your goat, is all. You can't taunt her. You can't even let on that you know what she is. Look how easily Reece got to her. I don't want him—or her—doing the same to you."

She stares at me over the lid of her cup, her eyes blank and cold. "I'm not helpless, you know." She slams the cup down.

"I know you're not." I sigh, leaning back, the sugary tea racing through my body, lifting my spirits.

So why isn't it doing the same for Abby?

"Is something . . . wrong?" I ask, watching her stare at a broken thumbnail for so long I'm surprised it's not fully healed by the time she finally looks up and answers me.

"You mean, something *other* than my ex-boyfriend being strung up in a cage and my ex-best friend having to write under the gun to save his life? You mean, something more than I have to watch my back against not one but two killer vampires who will be sitting less than three feet away from me for four out of seven periods all week? Not much, why?"

"*Ex*-best friend? What does that mean?"

"It means I'm mad at you. It means I know, and you're *not* forgiven!"

"*Know* what?" I ask, although I already suspect the answer, my face growing hot with the mounting suspense.

"Know this." She tosses her cell phone across the table at me.

I manage to catch it before it knocks over my cup. I hit the on button, and the screen flickers to life.

It's a text from Wyatt. Before I read the message, I check the time stamp—7:22 p.m. on the day he disappeared.

He must have written her on the way to the photo shoot, just after—I'm talking seconds after—leaving the coffee shop.

The message is brief and intimate and stings with betrayal:

*Abs, it finally hapnd. Just like u said it wld. Nora & I kssd. There wer firewks but . . . not bazooka blasts. You ok wit dat? Will c where it goz. Don't B angry. It had 2 happen sometime. W*

"What? Why? When?" My stomach somewhere on the floor, my eyes blurry, my butt half in, half out of my seat.

"The day it happened." She sighs, looking at me with new eyes that no longer smile. "So . . . why didn't *you* tell me? That night? When we had our big talk?"

"I wanted to. Really, I did. I just . . . What would you have rather heard? That I'd kissed Wyatt or that Bianca was a vampire?"

"How about both, Nora? I can take it, you know. I'm a big girl, remember?"

"It would have been nice if he'd told you *why* I kissed him," I say, avoiding eye contact. I always thought Abby would be okay if Wyatt and I ended up together. Like he said, it had to happen sometime. Did Abby not understand that? Or did she still have such strong feelings for him that it could cost us our very friendship?

"You mean besides primal, throbbing lust? You mean besides the fact that you've wanted to kiss him ever since you met him? Or how about the fact that you hated every minute of the two short months Wyatt and I dated? Which one is it, huh?"

"None of the above." I stare her down. "Actually, yeah, there *is* something other than that. Bianca was coming, I needed an alibi, he was there, and—"

"And rather than stopping to tie his shoe, or get a lash out of his eye, or help him with his homework, or show him how to work his cell phone, or a thousand and one other excuses you *could* have used, you chose to kiss him? My ex-boyfriend? To the point of fireworks? How could you?"

"But no bazookas," I point out miserably. "And very, very little fireworks." (Although I sure felt them.)

"Oh, well, you probably save your . . . bazookas for the second date!" She stands up, huffing, grabbing her backpack purse roughly off the back of her chair, where it snags. She yanks it free, and I can't tell which she's madder at: me for kissing Wyatt or her backpack purse for ruining her dramatic exit. (Sucks when real life doesn't follow a script, doesn't it?)

"You can't go, Abby. We said we'd stick together."

"You have writing to do," she says, looking down at my laptop. "And frankly, listening to you tap away at those keys all night would only make me want to smash your face in even more than I want to right now, which is pretty darn tempting as it is, so . . . Don't worry about me. A deal's a deal, right? You're doing your part. I'm on the sidelines. They're not going to try anything tonight."

I shake my head, powerless to argue with her fiery logic.

She storms out, swinging her arms into the dark.

I watch as she crosses the street alone, enters our dorm building alone, and disappears into the elevator—alone.

My laptop is calling, the big white page on the screen begging to be filled with words, countless words, each one another step closer to Wyatt's freedom.

# CHAPTER 17

*Scarlet Stain spits blood from her mouth, watching it pool on the dirty warehouse floor where she's being held captive by the man she's sworn to hunt down and eliminate.*

*The room is empty now, cavernous and vast, illuminated merely by large candles flickering in the corners. They light only the warehouse floor, dirty and littered with broken lightbulbs and dried-out rat carcasses.*

*She is comfortable; she is safe . . . but for how long?*

*Just outside the door, three of the count's most vicious vampire guards pace, just waiting for her to dare to try to escape. And how would she do that? They took her leather pants, her rubber boots, her white blouse, her backpack of weapons, her favorite dagger belt, even the monogrammed switchblade she always wore in her left sock.*

*She is bruised, battered, defenseless, and half-naked, crouching in the corner of her cage, a dented tray full of biscuit crumbs and refried beans her only sustenance for the last twelve hours straight.*

*But . . . but . . . they didn't find everything.*

*Sewn into the left strap of her sports bra is a simple pin, twice as thick as a sewing needle, half as sharp. In the right strap is its twin.*

*They are made of a special alloy, designed to elude metal detectors, even the portable wand kind Count Victus and his men waved over every inch of her half-naked body.*

*When the time is right, when the men are sleeping, when she has had enough, she will chew the bars from her bra and use them to pick the lock that has kept her in this cage for these past two days.*

*Her weapons are on a chair in the far corner of the room, twelve simple paces from where she sits. If she hurries, she can make it in four seconds flat. Once she has them, it will take her only twice that long to eliminate all three of the count's men.*

*But she will take her time with the count.*

*She will take all the time she needs to make sure his end is as painful as he deserves . . .*

I rub my eyes, look up from the scene, and stare at Wyatt, hanging against the bars of his cage across the endless warehouse floor.

Two days have passed, long days of writing, toiling, sleeping in this chair, lighting candles, chugging endless cans of Jolt Cola from the little fridge beneath my desk.

Say what you will about Reece, but the man has an eye for detail.

I blink, rub my eyes again, and look up past the oriental screens, the flickering candles, the grimy warehouse walls to the windows high above. The sun is rising.

Another day is here.

I look at the page count on my latest chapter: 127.

Two days more, and I can get to two hundred pages no

problem, finish off the book, and have Wyatt out of that cage.

Now if only Abby would return my texts.

I know she's mad at me, but this is serious.

Reece rouses from the corner where he's been napping, fully dressed, against two of the satin throw pillows. (I knew there was a reason there were so many of them.) He smiles and says, "Alas, I must take my leave. Big test in world cultures today. Wouldn't want to miss *that*."

I yawn, stretch, rise, and announce, "I'm going with you."

A cloud covers his face; he darts to a standing position. "I'd rather you write," he scolds, ever the impatient taskmaster.

"Just for a little while," I plead, all the while gathering my book bag, which stores the latest version of the manuscript on a flash drive. I defiantly stand in front of him. "I need to check on Abby."

"I told you she's fine." He sighs, rubbing his own face as if scrubbing it clean with his large, pale palms. "I told you yesterday morning and yesterday after school and last night, and I'm telling you now: Abby is fine. Stay here, finish the work, and—"

I wave the flash drive in front of his face, pat my laptop bag, and say, "I'll keep working—at school."

"Fine," he mumbles, leading the way out of the claustrophobic room that has become like a cell for us both.

I linger near Wyatt's cage on the way out, making sure the water pitcher at his feet is half full, the bowl of stew next to it empty, the crusty bread I insisted on (Wyatt's favorite) gone.

"You see," Reece says, impatient to get going, "I'm keeping my end of the bargain. He's being well taken care of. There will be no repercussions when at last the book is finished, he is let loose, and we are free of each other."

I look from Wyatt to Reece. "You mean that? This isn't

one of those deals where I write not just one book for you but one hundred and one? Where you're in my life forever, haunting my dreams, shadowing my every move?"

"Only if you want me to be." He inches near with those long, glistening fangs at the ready.

"Thanks," I say, turning before Wyatt can see the lurid display. "I prefer my men slightly less lethal, thanks."

We dash toward the Mercedes and get in. It cruises silently in the early light of dawn, taking us through the bleak streets that surround the warehouse.

I stifle a smile to learn that Reece's senses aren't defenseless. Sure, I wanted to check on Abby, absolutely. But there was an ulterior motive for the ride to school that day: the tinted windows make it difficult, but not impossible, to see the street names as we pass each one. I'd been careless, that first trip to see Abby at the café. Reese had insisted on driving me there, then picking me up later. I'd been so upset by the confrontation with Abby, I hadn't thought to follow my trail there or back. This time I would be smarter, calmer, more prepared. I had to be, just in case.

Straight up Rouse Street.

Left on Andover Lane.

Right on Oliver Street.

Another right on Principal Avenue.

Left on Archibald Street.

Right on Ninth Avenue.

Another right on Lavender Lane until we're on the recognizable surface streets of Beverly Hills at last.

I note each one while managing to look bored and distracted for Reece's benefit, memorizing the street names in order by making a little mnemonic device for myself, you know, the same way you remember the order of the planets: *Ralph and Ollie Partied All Night Long.*

I have no idea what good it will do me, but it makes me feel better to at least know the general area, just in case Reece decides to go back on his deal.

"What page are we on today?" he says, clearly breathing a sigh of relief as we pass Rodeo Drive and enter the nicer part of town again.

"Ninety-seven," I bluff, none too eager to give him any information he doesn't deserve.

"Not bad," he says, impressed.

What would he have thought if I'd told him I was actually thirty pages further along?

"So at this pace"—he does the mental math—"you'll be done by Monday morning."

"Or Monday afternoon, maybe Tuesday morning. Endings are the hardest," I warn, trying to buy myself a little time to formulate some kind of plan.

He nods knowingly. "Of course they are."

We glide into the student parking lot on a whisper, and I race for the door the minute he pulls into a spot.

I am out of the car and into the commons area before he turns off the ignition, racing to homeroom without stopping at my locker, without checking in with Principal Chalmers or my guidance counselor, without even using the bathroom.

Abby is there, safe and sound.

Safe and sound, that is, sitting cozily next to her new BFF, Bianca Ridley.

"Abby!" I gasp, glad that Mrs. Armbruster's not yet in the room.

"Nora!" she says giddily, her eyes, skin, and hair not her own.

Nothing is like it was. Nothing will ever be the same. Not now, not ever, not for any of them.

Her voice sounds slurred.

"What's going on here?" I ask, standing in front of them, hands on my hips, like a mother who's caught both her daughters sneaking in after curfew.

The class is nearly deserted, just a few early worms sitting in the corner, playing football with one of those triangular pieces of paper. They stand, their chairs sliding across the floor as they instinctively cluster in the farthest corner of the room from us.

"Wassup wit you?" Abby asks, making odd hand gestures, like some old-time hippie dancing to Jimi Hendrix in a muddy cow pasture.

"What? What does that even mean?" I snap, mad at myself for leaving Abby alone with Bianca and Reece.

"It means," Abby drolls, eyes and mouth half open, brain obviously completely shut down, "wassup wit—?"

"I *know* what it means." I sigh. "I just don't know why you're saying it."

Abby looks up at me, squinting, as if the light above my head is hurting her eyes, and then shakes her head like, *Dude, where's my brain?*

I watch her closely, beginning to tremble in earnest as I notice all the telltale signs: limp hair, pale skin, sweaty armpits, dry lips.

I reach for her hair, yank her head around, and see the bruised bite marks at the nape of her neck.

A wave of grief passes through me, so strong my knees literally tremble.

I look at Abby's wan face, her dazed eyes, and feel like

crying, like yelling, like tearing the room apart vampire by vampire.

And it's all my fault, every last bit of it.

I knew I should have kept Abby by my side, every minute of the day, every second.

How could I have been so stupid?

Now my best friend, my only friend, at this overachieving school for overachievers is gone forever—lured to the dark side with two quick bites from that witch Bianca.

All because I thought I could handle my business. All because I thought I was in control.

Nora Falcon, big, bad, best-selling writer.

"Trust me, Abby," I'd said. "I know what I'm doing. You'll be safe at school, with teachers and counselors and Principal Chalmers around."

"Trust me, Abby," I'd said. "The dorm is off limits. They won't try to get to you there. Why? Because Reece *said* so!"

And while I was tapping away at my breezy little keyboard, lulled into a creative state by flickering candles and the calming presence of two hundred silk pillows, Abby had been slowly transforming, morphing, dying—and then being reborn.

After a few seconds of awkwardly staring at the top of her desk while I inspect her bite marks, Abby mumbles something like, "Heywuzyougonnadowhy?" It starts out sounding vaguely pitiful, like when a kid wakes up in the middle of the night, but by the end she's almost snapping, barely hissing, like she's waking up to who she is, regardless of who I am.

It's not a pretty sound. It's an even worse sight.

Bianca reaches out a hand to stop me, and I jab it with a pencil, the point going all the way into her skin and drawing blood.

Suddenly Abby is on red alert, the earlier torpor gone, her

eyes bright and wide as she hisses, licking her lips.

I smack her—hard—on the cheek. "Snap out of it!"

Bianca hisses but not at the blood on her hand. She's hissing in my direction, her fangs just barely restrained enough to stay beneath her lips, her eyes a violent, raging yellow, her claws digging at the surface of her desk one more time.

She starts to stand, and I kick at the top of her desk, tipping it and her onto their sides. There's nothing Bianca hates worse than being embarrassed, let alone toppled.

Abby watches, looking at me with half-open eyes, as if trying to recognize me. Or remember me.

Bianca doesn't struggle long, and the chair is but a minor inconvenience. She snaps to attention and roars, slipping through the desk's arms and legs and desktop like a salamander emerging from a crack in the sidewalk. Once up and out of the desk, she reaches my side in a blink.

She has me by the throat and up against the wall before I know what's happening. My feet are two, maybe three, inches off the ground and kicking against the cinder-block wall as I gasp for air.

The kids clustered in the corner are standing up now, their faces pale and panicked, half of them looking tempted to rush to my side, the other half trying to climb through the wall at their backs. I don't blame them for hanging back; I wish I were that smart!

I kick out with both feet, connecting with Bianca's waist and sending her thick red belt to the floor.

Bianca only presses harder, her face a mask of venom and bliss, her smile sticky across her fangs as they begin to jut, farther and farther, out of her upper jaw.

"Two seconds," she hisses, licking her lips and eyeing the

soft, white meat of my throat. "Two seconds is all it would take me to end you, Nora Falcon!" Her hand presses even tighter against my throat. I swallow harder than I ever have, see the room go faint, then tan, then gray . . . then all is black.

Black, like Bianca's eyes.

Black, like Reece's heart.

Black, like Abby's unwritten—but quite doomed—future.

# CHAPTER 18

I come to in my writing chamber, on a bed of huge satin throw pillows. Candles flicker in every available space, the jumble of black and red décor assaulting my eyes.

I gasp, reaching for my throat, still sore, and cough for probably two minutes straight. Tears run down my face, but there's no way to control them. They gather on my upper lip and get coughed away. Just breathing feels like it should take an act of Congress. What I wouldn't give for a cough drop!

I wonder for a minute if I'm paralyzed, if Bianca made good on her threat and snapped my neck. But no. I can wriggle my toes and feel my butt, which is sore and quite asleep after who knows how long of lying in this room.

The warehouse is empty . . .

No, that's not quite right.

As I lift my tired arms and rub my dry eyes, sounds start to emerge from the darkness just beyond the screens.

Unnatural sounds.

I listen closely and can just make them out: scraping and clattering and then a triumphant squeal.

I look past the open entry between the screens, blink my eyes clear, then blink again. Abby has just snatched a rat—you read that right, a rodent—from under a discarded hard hat, dented and rusty with age, and is sinking her new fangs into its rough, trembling hide.

"Abby!" I shout.

But my best friend's eyes are glazed over in ecstasy, and she's not taking any messages from mere mortals anymore—not when there are living rodents to devour instead.

At her side, Bianca kicks the hard hat away in disappointment. "No fair. Beginner's luck."

At their feet lie several discarded rat carcasses, all fresh, all quite sucked dry, scattered like crushed beer cans at a tailgate party.

"You guys are sick." I struggle to my feet. "I hope you both catch vampire rabies and—"

From the chair at my desk Reece urges, "Be still," in a voice that leaves no room for argument. "You lied to me," he says calmly, tapping a thick stack of printed pages sitting next to my closed laptop. "You said you'd only written ninety-seven pages. I count over a hundred and twenty-seven here."

"*You* lied to *me*." I stand on wobbly legs, glaring at him but pointing toward the opening in the screen with one trembling finger. "You said Abby was quite safe. Look at her now. Is that what *safe* looks like to *you*?"

We both turn our heads to find Abby and Bianca fighting over a fresh rat.

"Ah, but I didn't lie, sweet Nora." He turns away from my BFF and pierces me with those dark-chocolate eyes. "I wager this is the safest Abby has ever been in her entire life."

I hate to admit he has a point.

"But why?" I ask, edging closer, not wanting her to hear the desperation, the failure, in my panic-stricken voice. "I've done everything you asked. *Everything.* I'm not just on schedule; I'm ahead of schedule. I'm writing your book, using your word list, in all the right places. Check it. It's all right there in your hands. Look for yourself."

"Your point?" His tongue slithers across a fang.

"My point, Reece, is that you didn't have to *turn* her." My voice cracks, the tears fall. "She's nothing to you. She's everything to me. Everything, and now that's all gone."

"She was becoming . . . a liability," he explains without sympathy or concern.

"Abby? Little Abby? Vegetarian, pacifist, wimpus extraordinaire Abby? A liability? How?"

"She hated us," he spits, finally showing some emotion. "She hated Bianca, hated me for turning Bianca. I heard her twice in class talking about vampires. Apropos of nothing, mind you. Just, 'Blah, blah, blah; by the way, did you know vampires go to school here?' What was I supposed to do? No one believed her, thankfully, but I couldn't risk her saying the right words at the right time to the right person and finding an ally at Nightshade Academy."

I shake my head, tears flowing freely now. I try to make my voice sound steely as I say, "You shouldn't have done that," but I fail and whimper instead.

"Really?" he says, suddenly interested. "And why's that?"

And so I play it, the only card I have left, slapping it on the table. "It's done," I say, shoulders drooping. "I'm out. You lied, so it's over. Forget you. Forget your stupid book. We're done."

He stands, seeming taller than ever before.

I inch back, away from him, but the room is so small there's nowhere else to go.

He stands erect, his fists clenched, his eyes as black as night, his fangs glistening like diamonds in the flickering candlelight as they threaten to literally erupt from his upper jaw in a spasm of pure rage. "Nora, you try my patience. You really do. Bianca? Abby? My dear, let me assure you, they are just the beginning. Wyatt is next. Do you no longer care about your friend?"

"I care. I just don't believe you anymore. I think the minute I'm through with that book, the moment I type the last word on the last page, you'll kill him, and then you'll kill me, so why bother? You might as well kill us both now, because I'm not typing another single word for you. Ever!"

He smiles now, suspecting it's an empty threat, perhaps even knowing so. "Believe me or don't believe me, but know this. Unless you start writing immediately, I will relish turning Wyatt, drive straight to Nightshade Academy, and run amok. Blood will fill the halls, the classrooms, the very gym. I will turn everyone you've ever known, everyone you've sat next to, in front of, or behind.

"Every teacher you've ever had, your principal, your coach, your counselor, the janitor—they will all be vampires before you can say, 'I shouldn't have threatened Reece.' Hundreds will lose their lives, all because of your stubbornness. Generations will be lost, futures ruined, all because you choose to grow petty and tiresome."

He moves so close, so fast, I barely have time to flinch. From a few feet away he is suddenly face-to-face with me, so that I can admire every inch of his curving, elaborate fangs, watch them glisten in the firelight as he sneers at me maliciously.

"*Kill* you? Why, I wouldn't dream of it! It will be my undying duty to force you to watch the mayhem you've caused, and every tear you spill will be like nectar to me, dear girl. Your pain will be my ultimate reward, and trust me: your pain will be intense, historic . . . *epic*."

He takes one step toward the opening of the small room, motioning toward Wyatt's unconscious body in chains.

"Shall I begin, Nora? Shall I get to work . . . or shall you?"

I shiver, dry my tears, and sit.

He smiles, turning ugly with each corner of upturned lip, with each visible tooth. Leaving the room, he hisses over his shoulder, "There is work to do. I suggest you get to it."

And of course, that's exactly what I do.

# CHAPTER 19

I find the code at exactly 3:19 a.m.

The vampires, all three of them, Abby included, are out in the vacant lot that borders the warehouse, snacking on field mice, gophers, rabbits, raccoons, bobcats, and who knows what else they can scrounge up with their nasty night vision and creepy claws. I can hear them, hissing triumphantly each time they snag another field creature from its burrow.

Abby's voice is particularly grating. I'd expected her to turn gradually, to at least retain some last vestiges of humanity until the bloodlust conquered her completely, but she's worse than the rest. She's like that Catholic schoolgirl who's a goody-goody until her seventeenth birthday, and the first time her folks go away for the weekend, she throws the house party to end all house parties, doing a striptease while singing karaoke, sucking body shots off burly jocks, and out-tramping the tramps.

I know Abby's moods: surly, quiet, thankful, generous, and giddy. She's in a giddy mood now, times 817! She catches a rat, breaks its neck, and starts chowing down. It's like Christmas, New

Year's Eve, her birthday, and her last *Zombie Diaries* wrap party all rolled into one.

I don't know which sound disgusts me more: the yelps of the furry victims or the slurping of the inhuman victors.

Meanwhile, I am on page 148, almost there, nearing the finish line, with Scarlet Stain and Count Victus trapped in their third epic battle scene of the book.

My readers typically insist on a minimum of four fight scenes, so I have one to go, but I'm saving it for the big finale.

I'm stuck, as usual, trying to find a place for word #148: *dark*.

It shouldn't be that hard to place: line fourteen, word eight, just as Reece taught me.

Problem is, my brain is fried!

I'm scrolling back through the previous two pages, trying to see how far I'll have to go back to change this day scene into night—I should have read ahead on the list to know in advance before I committed myself to sunshine instead of moonlight—when I notice the two previous words highlighted in yellow for Reece to see: *the* and *in*.

Over the boisterous sounds of garden creature hunting, I think to myself, *Hmm, that's a little odd . . .*

So I scroll back even more for the next three words: *kept, be,* and *shall.*

I hear the vampires sacrifice another field creature. I cringe and grab the word list from next to my laptop for a closer look. Using a sharpened pencil from an oversized porcelain cup shaped like a Buddha on the left-hand corner of my desk (that Reece, he thinks of everything), I circle the latest six words: *dark the in kept be shall.*

My eyes, dry and tired from another twelve-hour day of writing, blur, then clear, then blur again. But even with my constant, exhausted, overworked blur-a-vision, I can tell *something* isn't right. These six words, when strung together like this, don't just sound like random words. They sound like a phrase—an odd phrase, one that doesn't make any sense, but a phrase nonetheless.

Is it?

Is Reece trying to talk?

To someone else?

Inside my book?

But how?

And what does it mean?

I look at the words, trying to decipher any kind of recognizable phrase, anything at all, my eyes blurring, and that's when I flash back to when Abby got her wisdom teeth taken out last year.

It was an outpatient procedure at one of the best dentists in Beverly Hills, but since none of our parents were ever around, I had to take Abby there, wait, and then take her home, making sure she got painkiller and antinausea prescriptions on the way. Not that I'm complaining; we signed away our rights to having parental supervision when we entered Nightshade Academy for Exemplary Boys and Girls.

Naturally, the dentist's office she chose was typical Beverly Hills. They didn't even call it a dentist's office; they called it a Surgical Smile Spa. (No, I'm *not* making that up.)

After grinding two of her wisdom teeth to a pulp and yanking them out one by one, the dentist placed Abby in one of the recovery rooms, which was bigger—and nicer—than our dorm suite at Nightshade Academy (and much bigger and much nicer than the trailer I grew up in back in Barracuda Bay).

There was a gurgling fountain in one corner, a heated,

vibrating, leather recliner for Abby to doze off her anesthesia in, a matching one for me to read magazines in, a full soda-and-water bar, snacks, aromatherapy candles, and ambient music oozing from a tiny Bose sound system in the corner. Enya, I think it was. Or Sade. Something soothing and sensual like that.

Anyway, when Abby woke up, she was still a little loopy from the anesthesia, and man, was she *thirsty*.

The nurse had warned me—vehemently—not to give her any water, but Abby didn't know that. She also didn't know how to say the word *water* anymore. At least, not while still coming out of the anesthesia. Everything she said came out garbled, upside down, or backward.

At one point she said, "Fountain the from it take." She was slurring her words, sounding mushy, so it was hard to comprehend. But she just kept repeating it, like you do when someone's hard of hearing, even though if that person can't hear you the first time, what makes you think he'll hear you on the one hundred first time?

At one point I thought she said, "Ferngully is a lake."

Then it sounded like, "Rockefeller's on the take."

I made the international scrunched-up face for *Huh?* and she slapped her thighs, repeating herself over and over—"Fountain the from it take"—until the nurse came back into the recovery room, checked her out, gave me her prescriptions to be filled, and released us.

The walk to the car was confusing and probably painful, the sunlight hitting her in the face. She winced as I slid her into the passenger seat of her black Lexus. That shut her up, and she quit going on and on about "Fountain the from it take."

I didn't think twice about it until I was coming back to the car, her two prescriptions in hand, and Abby was sitting there in the passenger seat, clear-eyed and frowning at me, her face pale, her eyes quite bright.

"Why didn't you give me the drink I asked for?" she said, arms crossed.

"What drink? When?"

"Back in the recovery room," she said very clearly. "I asked you for a drink out of the fountain."

As I pulled out into traffic and hugged the right lane, I said, "No, you didn't. You said 'Fountain the from it take.'"

She slapped her thigh again and said, "No, I was saying, 'Take it from the fountain!' But I didn't want the nurse to hear, so I said it backward. Gosh, some BFF *you* are. I could have died of thirst in there. What if we were on some super-duper spy mission trying to save the world and you missed my code? We need to work on that."

We never did, of course. Abby's codes were mostly in her mind, and we'd certainly never agreed beforehand to speak backward, sideways, Pig Latin, or French after her surgery!

The memory fresh in my mind, the sounds of dying field mice ringing in my ears, the vampire's bloodlust making me sick to my gullet, I open a fresh document and type in the phrase as it's found in the book: *dark the in kept be shall.*

They sit there at the top of that blank page and, reading them from back to front, I suddenly see what Reece is really trying to say: *shall be kept in the dark.*

I stare at the words, play with them 101 different ways, but only *this* way makes sense.

It's no coincidence. It can't be.

Reece isn't forcing me to write a book about vampires.

He's writing a book *for* vampires.

And he's using me to do it.

But why?

# CHAPTER 20

*At hour seventeen on the seventh day of the winter solstice in the year of our Lord 2017 shall we meet on the banks of Lake Hammer in west Texas for the purposes of conveying this year's business to include a restructuring of the ruling party and also lifting the ban on turning male vampires it has come to the Council's attention that several members of the Rothchild clan have been breaking the ban in the decade since our last conclave the Council wishes to remind our international brothers and sisters that they should be in country for ten days prior to conclave to avoid any unnecessary delays it is very important that all or as many of us as possible attend the conclave and spread the new bylaws passed to those who cannot attend for whatever reason all nonvampire friends and family shall be kept in the dark about conclave it is to last four full days and on the fifth day as is our custom we shall feast the town of Hammer has a population of thirty thousand which I'm sure you'll agree is more than enough if we share until then rest and travel safely in good time.*

*This* is what the words on the spreadsheet say when you read them backward.

This is the code Reece is using in the fifth Better off Bled book.

Why he forced me to write the book.

Why he stalked me for who knows how long, hunted me down, enrolled in my school, charmed me, made one friend a vampire and the other a victim and *ruined my life.*

The words on the spreadsheet aren't just random keywords he's using to boost my book sales or further some secret cause. They aren't even random at all. It's a coded message buried in the book, one word on each page, so cleverly hidden you couldn't find it, not in a million years, if you didn't know two very important things:

1. The code itself
2. The fact that you had to read it backward

As the vampires finish their hunting trip, I print the coded message, fold it, and slip it inside a rarely used pocket deep inside my leather messenger bag.

Then I stare at the latest page of the book and wonder why.

Why me?

It's not just because I write vampire books.

Dozens, hundreds, maybe even thousands of writers do that.

But he doesn't care about the guts of the book. The plot, the details, the pacing, the tone, the theme—all those things I've been working so hard to finesse since he kidnapped Wyatt and brought me to this place—mean little to him. Mean nothing.

He gave me that admittedly juicy story line only to throw me off track. What he wanted was a warm body—a human body—to sit at this laptop day and night until the manuscript was through, until each word of the code was safely buried in the guts of this book, right where he wanted them. Just as planned.

What did Reece say, way back when, when I asked him if he was going to turn me?

"Of course not," he said. "You would be useless to me then."

Useless.

To.

Me.

It made me feel safe at the time, like the folks with immunity on *Survivor*, but now I know it's yet another clue, just like the backward words he's using for the code.

Digging deeper, racking my memory, weak and confused as it is, I flash back to when Reece called me a liar. When he called my bluff about the page count. He was sitting in this very chair, the laptop right in front of him, and yet he printed the pages and read them that way.

Why?

At the time I figured he was just old school—like Mrs. Armbruster or some other more technically challenged teachers at Nightshade—and preferred reading print to online, but now? I stand up, step back from the desk, and look at my laptop.

What is it about my laptop Reece doesn't like?

It can't be the shiny cover, because he wouldn't care if he couldn't see his reflection, and I already know he's a vampire, so . . . what else?

It can't be the electricity, because he uses electric stuff all the time: his car, his portable razor, the fridge under my desk where he stocked all that Jolt Cola that turned me into a lean, mean writing machine.

So what else?

What else would make him print the pages instead of reading them off the screen?

Why in the world would an impatient thug like Reece waste all that time and energy waiting for 120-plus pages to print out when he could just as easily open my laptop and read it on that nice, big, wide . . . glowing . . . screen?

That's it: the *screen*!

But not just any screen: the glowing screen.

My laptop was open when I left it sitting there untended, and he caught me in a lie.

But first he closed it.

I think of Bianca and how often she used her cell phone before Reece turned her. You couldn't get that witch *off* the thing, day or night. Now she never uses it at all.

Come to think of it, Reece doesn't even seem to own a cell phone. I never saw him text or call anyone.

I hear them outside, laughing, high off their bloodlust, sated from their kills, chattering as dawn approaches. They stumble into the warehouse like drunks off a three-day bender, arm in arm, shoulder to shoulder, their skin alive, their dark eyes liquid and all-seeing.

Bianca kicks off her shoes, Reece pulls off his boots, but Abby leaves on her sparkly pink sneakers to dance around the vast empty warehouse, drunk on quarts of fresh blood, tempting Wyatt in his cage with a blood-splattered hoodoo dance.

I shut my laptop tight and stand near it. "Abby!" I shout, seeing an opportunity to test my theory. "Quit teasing him like that. Abby, come here!"

Reece looks up, sees me standing there, defenseless, no weapons, no training, just another mortal bookworm at his mercy. He ignores me and goes back to polishing the dirt off his boots by the front door.

Abby saunters over, haughty, strong, immortal, and asks with a sigh, "What *is* it, Nora? Can't you see I'm *busy*?"

"Busy doing *what*? Sucking the life out of field mice? Have you already forgotten you're a vegetarian?"

"I've forgotten a lot of things," she says, eyes dark, skin supple, fangs plumping out her lips in a way that makes her look seductive and unwholesome. Always Abby has been the safe one, the only starlet in town who hasn't been to rehab or jail. Now, though she still looks like Abby, she looks like . . . Evil Abby. She may be prettier, but she's lost that human touch, that grace and gentleness and humor that drew me to her like I was drawn to Wyatt. "Not that you'd care," she says, looking with disdain at my desk, my pillows, my flickering candles.

I shake my head. "I'm sorry, Abby, for what's happened to you."

"Sorry? I should thank you, deserting me like that, leaving me all alone to fend for myself. I never knew how strong I was until Bianca released me from my human bondage!"

"Human bondage?" I snort. "I don't know what's worse: Vampire Abby or your last *Zombie Diaries* script."

Abby leans in close, right where I want her. "I'm worse, Nora. I'm *much* worse!"

"Yeah, sure. It's just, I wanted you to see what I've written—"

Before she can turn to avoid the light, I flip open the laptop cover, filling my office space with its bright white glow, like a laser beam pointed straight at her face. She's stuck in its twenty-one-inch glare, her eyes instantly shutting, her beautiful skin searing, her vocal cords shrieking as she ducks to avoid the light, then falls to the ground.

I quickly shut the laptop and put it back on the desk, feeling all kinds of guilty but just as relieved.

I know the secret now. I know Reece's weakness.

Abby is mewling by the time Reece and Bianca rush to her aid, smoke rising from the floor where she lies, curled in a fetal position, clutching her steaming cheeks.

"What did you do?" Reece demands as he helps her up.

I see the fresh scars on her face, raw like hamburger meat.

"N-n-nothing," I stammer, acting clueless. "I just wanted her to read my latest chapter. I mention her and thought she'd like it."

"Print it, Nora!" Reece shouts without further explanation or, for that matter, suspicion. "Next time, print it for her . . . for any of us!"

He takes Abby into the next room, calming her with gentle words as Bianca follows reluctantly.

Behind them, I smile for the first time in days.

# CHAPTER 21

I finish the book at noon, saving it all kinds of ways and backing it up on three separate flash drives Reece has brought me in a small Office Warehouse bag.

The vampires have entirely given up on the pretense of going to school by now, sleeping off their bloodlust in the darkest corner of the warehouse, well behind Wyatt's cage, where the light from the ceiling's broken windows never seems to reach.

I sit at my laptop, but I'm not using it. Instead, I'm keying the coded message—all two hundred words of it—into my cell phone as a draft.

But that's not enough.

I know how lethal Reece is, how much of the predator's blood roils beneath his dignified human skin.

He'll find some way to steal my phone, smash it, destroy it. I'll need backup for this to work, and plenty of it.

Abby's backpack is near the front door where she dropped it after strolling in after school the other day.

Wyatt's bag, dusty and untended, is on a wobbly wooden bar stool just outside his cage.

I hear the vampires dozing. Their closed eyes are dark under raised hoodies as they huddle together for warmth, like quivering, hairless beavers in a dam. Their breath is heavy and redolent of copper. How could Reece spend so much time polishing the field off his boots but not wipe the blood of the field mice off his lips? Gross.

I tiptoe to Abby's bag first, avoiding every broken lightbulb and rat bone in my path.

Or, at the very least, trying to.

It takes forever, because each time I land on a rust flake, I have to stop and look up to see if one of the vampires has risen. They haven't.

Not yet, anyway.

Abby's backpack is full of her old life. Blue rewrite pages from her latest *Zombie Diaries* movie. Black-and-white head shots of human Abby looking young, scrubbed, and innocent. Endless tubes of her favorite lip gloss. *Zombie Diaries* buttons and bumper stickers to give to the freshmen. The fabric journal I gave her last Christmas, which she never wrote anything in but kept anyway. I find her pink cell phone in a zipper pocket, next to $138 in cash and a stack of her talent agent's foil business cards (just in case).

I slip the phone into my back jeans pocket, looking up to find the vampires still snoozing.

Well, that was the easy part (if you could call taking forty-five minutes to walk twelve feet easy).

Now to stumble into the lions' den.

Wyatt's cage squats in the middle of the warehouse, equidistant between my lavish writing room and the squalid corner where the vampires slumber.

The light is bad. My eyes are blurry from overwriting for

the last week straight. My head is pounding. My hips, back, and neck ache from sitting too long and now stumbling so slowly over every tiny obstacle that might possibly make noise.

I know I have enough cell phones. Two is plenty, but if I've learned one thing about vampires—well, fictional ones anyway—enough is never enough.

I reach Wyatt's cage without crunching any bulbs or bottles or bones, peeling open his satchel slowly to find his life spelled out in empty gum wrappers and scraps of paper, on which are written scores of girls' phone numbers, their loopy script filled with *i*'s dotted with hearts—some of them even extra-special hearts with eyes and a smile drawn inside—and names written in pink ink and spelling out tempting lady names like *Amber* and *Audrina* and *Saffron* and *Sage*.

Cad!

His phone is at the very bottom, natch (God forbid I found it before stumbling across all those scented scraps of paper), and I'm so relieved to see it, I reach for it instinctively, forgetting how the On button is on the side, a feature Wyatt was endlessly complaining about and I was endlessly telling him to go exchange it for.

I feel it vibrating in my hand and know the sound is coming, but there's nothing I can do except toss it into Wyatt's cage and hope Reece falls for the scam.

Wyatt stirs, eyes wide and fearful until he sees it's me. "Nora," he whispers, his voice hoarse, and at that very moment his phone springs to life with a telltale *deedle-dwi-doo-doo-hummm* tone as the screen begins to glow while coming to rest just at his feet. "What? What are you doing?" he hisses as the vampires rise.

"Just trust me, OK?"

Their feet rustle against the bare warehouse floor, crunching every bone and broken beer bottle in their path.

"Just . . . follow my lead."

"Some lead!" he shouts, somehow finding the time—and the energy—to smile.

# CHAPTER 22

They are on me in a hot second, all three of them cornering me in the shadow of Wyatt's cage. I do a good job of cowering before their looming shadows and glistening fangs.

Their anger is a living thing, seething out of their mouths, burning in their eyes, oozing from their blood-soaked pores.

Even Abby looks outraged, and I wonder why, because certainly she can't know about the code yet or the conclave or the thirty thousand poor residents of Lake Hammer, Texas.

Maybe it's just me she hates, as if I'd blame her.

Reece reaches me first, hulking in front of me larger than life, his chest broader, his arms longer, his fangs already protruding. "Why aren't you at your desk?" he shouts.

Bianca appears at my left side, hissing, crouched like an animal ready to pounce. She pokes me, and her hard, sharp nails scratch my soft, mortal skin.

Abby is on my right, circling, reaching out, hissing.

I hiss back, just to show her I know who she is and hate her for it, even as my heart breaks for her. "I'm done!" I stare down Reece. "Done with your stupid book. And your stupid code. I hope you're happy!"

He smiles to hear the good news, then remembers why he's here. "So what was that *noise*?"

I frown, pretending I don't know the answer and doing it badly. "W-w-what noise?" I ask, flitting a glance toward Wyatt's cage that they're sure to catch.

They do.

"His phone," Abby shouts, pointing to it proudly. "He must have had his phone in this bag, and she was trying to get it."

"Thanks, Abby." I sigh, trying to sound hurt.

"Thanks, *Nora*," she hisses, leaning in. "Thanks for leaving me all alone, unprotected against these guys! What should I have done, Nora? Give up, or adapt? Weren't you the one who told me to be *strong*? Who made me promise to be strong, just before you let me walk across the street from the café alone so you could write your precious book?"

Reece and Bianca ignore our little catfight as they struggle to retrieve the phone from Wyatt's cage.

"*My* precious book? I was writing so fast only to help Wyatt. All I needed you to do was keep your mouth shut and stay out of trouble. I told you to play along. I warned you not to blab your big stinkin' mouth about Bianca, let alone Reece. But oh, no, you couldn't do that, could you? You just couldn't leave well enough alone."

"What do you mean?" she asks, sounding almost . . . human.

"He told me, Abby. Reece told me how you were going around school, blabbing to anyone who would listen about how Bianca was a vampire, about how—"

"Did *not*!" she shouts, shoving me so hard I literally fly back, landing on a pile of desiccated rats, which fortunately break my fall (albeit in the absolutely grossest possible way).

Reece shouts, "Abby, we need her here, where we can see her. Quit treating her like a play toy and drag her back."

But I'm up now, scrambling in reverse as she advances, desperate to get to my room, my pillows, my desk.

She ignores him, angry now, stomping, reaching me quickly, fangs protruding, eyes yellow, face a mask of hurt and shame. "I never said a *word*, Nora. I knew how much was on the line, how much danger we were in. I showed up to that school every day, sat near those two . . . two . . . *monsters* every day, trembling for fifty minutes each time, and never said a word. She came and broke into our dorm. Bianca bit me without warning, for no reason, just because she *could*. And you know who sent her? Reece did. I never blabbed. To anybody. Ever."

Her fangs tremble, face freshly healed from my little computer screen experiment the other day. She's closing in, licking her lips, hungry for my blood, my pulsing veins.

"Then I'm sorry, Abby."

That stops her short. "For what?"

"For this!" I say, yanking open the laptop and shoving it in her face.

# CHAPTER 23

Abby is still screaming, lying in a pile of gore and smoke beneath my desk, curled up like an infant, clawing at the skin that sizzles and boils above her neck.

Bianca screeches like a wild thing, racing across the room toward me, but I'm ready, the laptop yanked free from its power cord, charged up, and wired to last 4.5 whole hours of vampire-sizzling good times (if *I* can last that long, that is).

I hold the laptop like a shield, its white-hot glow reaching out inches in front of me in the gloomy warehouse light: the biggest, fattest, UV-spitting spotlight I can find.

Bianca stops too soon to get the full sizzle effect that Abby got but not short enough to emerge unscathed. Her chin catches fire as I shove the laptop toward her, but she's strong enough—older and wiser and meaner than Abby by two whole vampire days (which is probably like two whole weeks in human time)—and knocks the laptop free from my hands.

It lands in a pile of pillows, unbroken but facedown, and it won't do me any good from all the way over there. I scramble after it, but she's too fast, too strong, and pins me with a hard sneaker on my soft elbow.

Here's the thing they never tell you in books or show you in movies: pain hurts. It really does; I'm not gonna lie. Her shoe on my little wimpy arm is like a hot poker in my eye. It stings and grinds and threatens to break me at any minute.

What's more, she knows it, and she likes it. Bianca grinds her foot into the soft flesh of my arm.

Already I'm thinking, *Don't let her break my typing fingers!*

I squirm on all fours, scrambling forward until she puts the other foot on my butt and shoves me down. And that hurts too. Everything she does hurts, and she knows it, and that's why she's doing it. I feel the breath get knocked out of me, feel the bruises start to swell on my arm, feel the catch of a pillow zipper against my chest, and *that* hurts too!

I flip over, panicking, anything to avoid the pain, kicking at her groin, her thighs, backing her away from me, if only momentarily.

Somehow, it's enough.

I grab Abby's phone from my back pocket as Bianca turns to sink her fangs into my belly. The bright glow from Abby's touch screen pierces Bianca's hide like a cattle brand. Not content to watch her stumble away, I clutch her throat where the first sizzle burns and shove the lighted touch screen against her skin. It sears her all over, as if it's a hot iron in some medieval torture chamber. Her skin is falling off in big, square clumps by the end, like a cheap Halloween mask coming apart after a long night of trick-or-treating. I see bone in places, sinew in others—her face, neck, chest, arms like a patchwork blanket of herself.

She quivers on the floor, whimpering in a heap, and I'm not done yet.

I've watched this scene in too many movies to walk away

from a wounded vampire and think nothing will come of it. Bianca is wounded, yes, but still breathing, and I just can't let that ride.

I look around for a weapon, for anything, and see the thing that's gotten me in all this trouble in the first place: my desk. Big, solid, with four sturdy legs.

I kick it to the floor with a great smashing thunder, then stomp one of the legs until it breaks off.

Bianca snuffles, whimpers, but doesn't move. It's like she knows what's coming but is powerless to stop it.

There is no time to whittle the broken desk leg down into a sharper point, but the jagged edge looks just spikey enough. It'll have to do.

I grab the other end in both hands, stand over Bianca like a ditch digger with his shovel, and without hesitation—without a second thought—without guilt or remorse, I plunge the stake straight down into her chest. It cracks a few ribs and jabs into her heart on the first try. She erupts like a fireball, like a giant M-80 going off in the world's biggest toilet. The huge ash plume explodes around me, covering the entire office in bone and flames and charcoal briquettes that look suspiciously like fingers and toes.

With ashes flying around me, a great black dust cloud of once-human flesh and bone, I turn triumphantly to face Reece, only to find him standing inside Wyatt's cage. Not outside—inside.

Wyatt is free now, his shackles loosened, his phone in pieces under Reece's imported leather soles, but he is far from liberated.

Reece has him shoved up against the rusty metal bars, the surface rubbing harshly against his smooth cheeks, his nose bent and ready to break at the slightest application of pressure from behind. Reece holds him by the shoulders, his face alight with glee, his gaze transfixed on the smoking remains of his latest acolytes.

"Well done, my dear. To think, a mortal—a measly mortal—has bested two of my own flesh. I am truly impressed."

"Me too," I say, inching forward, my hand on the preloaded cell phone in my pocket.

"Careful," he says as I pull it free but aim the glow at myself. He wraps his free hand tighter around the back of Wyatt's neck, just in case.

"Forget him," Wyatt says, fully awake now. "Run, Nora. Get out of here!"

I ignore Wyatt, though it pains me to do so, and stare at Reece. "I'm impressed with the simplicity of your code."

He doesn't even blink. "What code?"

I look at the text message draft I keyed in earlier, queued up and ready to send to every media contact in my address book—and trust me, after four *New York Times* best sellers, they're all in there.

GNN.

RSNBC.

Satellite Network News.

The tabloids.

DMZ.com.

Even *Teen Talk*.

One push of the Send button, and the whole world knows where the next conclave will be.

"This one," I say, reading the first few lines aloud from my glowing phone screen: "At hour seventeen on the seventh day of the winter solstice in the year of our Lord 2017 shall we meet on the banks of Lake Hammer in west Texas."

I stop reading, scan his face, and see the waves of rage wash over him. He is speechless, but I know it won't last.

"So what does it mean, Reece? Why this elaborate code? Who reads it, if you guys can't even answer a cell phone, can't even glance at a computer monitor?"

"That's just it." He smiles, loosening his grip on Wyatt the slightest bit. "We can't use your cell phones, can't read your computer monitors, can't even watch TV. Not that we're missing much, from what I can tell. It's the UV rays, of course. They're as bad as the sun. Worse, in some cases. So we must rely, alas, on the printed page."

I mull it over, see the possibilities.

"You mean, this is an . . . invitation?"

He nods.

"To . . . conclave?"

"Very good," he says, and I still can't tell if he's mocking—or praising—me. "*Very* good."

"Care to elaborate?"

"Not really." He sighs, opening his free hand to reveal the flash drives I carefully hid around my work space. "But now that the book is done, the code is in place, the printers stand at the ready, and you won't survive the day—why not? You see, Nora dear, every ten years the remaining twenty-five thousand or so vampires on this planet gather at something known as a conclave.

"It's a gathering, traced back to ancient times when we numbered but a few. The code you so deftly deciphered is, in fact, an invitation. Every vampire on the planet will converge on this tiny Texas town, where we'll meet for four days, conducting business, passing judgment, enacting laws, dealing punishment, and then we'll feast on the good people of Lake Hammer. It's a delicious plan, also passed down through the ages. We don't just eliminate the witnesses; we feed on them. Two birds, as they say, I believe?"

"So let me get this straight. You read my books, liked them—"

"Heavens no." The truth I long suspected finally comes out. "They're complete rubbish. However, they are popular and have now been translated into thirty-four languages, precisely the ones we'll need to reach our international brethren. So, please, don't flatter yourself."

"Of course not." I groan. "The point being, you came here, stalked me, tricked me into writing your book and implanting this code, and now . . . what? All the vampires will know to read it? How do you let them know if you can't communicate via e-mail or phone or computer?"

"The books, stupid. Every vampire buys every vampire book ever published, just in case. Why do you think the ridiculous things *sell* so well? We read the first few pages. If there's no code, we toss the things, sell them on eBay, or better still, burn them. That way no mortal can know which book the code will be in, and no one will *ever* know."

I shake my head. "Amazing. So just how long has this little 'system' been going on?"

He smirks, still holding fast to Wyatt's neck as he pockets the three precious flash drives.

"Ever heard of a little book called *Dracula*?"

"What?"

"Of course we used a different code back then, so good luck solving *that* one after all these years, but yes . . . The first-ever book about vampires was also used as an invitation to the first conclave. So if you think I'm going to let some teenage wannabe writer ruin our first conclave in a decade, you have another think coming."

I hold up the phone again, tempted to shine it in his direction, but he hides behind Wyatt.

"So what if the plans for the conclave change?" I ask. "How would you alert all the vampires in time?"

"We couldn't, you fool! I just told you, no one knows the addresses of every vampire on the planet. It would be too dangerous if the authorities were to catch us and break one of us. We are anonymous and care to keep it that way. Conclave is a duty, and we keep it religiously."

Now I smile at my phone. "So if I were to, say, type in the message—the entire message—in a text message, and send it to every media outlet in this country, you and the entire vampire race would pretty much be hosed, right? There'd be no way to alert everyone in time, and—"

"Nora," Reece says, desperate now and peering over Wyatt's head with eyes so dark they might have been underground. "If you even so much as threaten such a whimsy, I will literally tear your friend here apart and feed him to you, ounce by ounce. Then I will make it my life's mission to hunt down anyone you've ever known and kill them so slowly they will beg to die. Beg to die, that is, right in front of your eyes."

"How ya gonna do that"—I poise my finger over the Send button—"with the authorities hunting you down and—?"

I feel cold flesh shoving my hand away. The phone hits the floor, where a familiar size-eight sparkly pink sneaker smashes it to smithereens.

Reece smiles. "Abby, wonderful."

I turn to face my assailant and slap the sear marks on her face. As she screams, I turn, grabbing the metal bars, shaking them in my fists, pleading with Reece. "I didn't do it. The secret stops here. Take me! Let him go! I finished the book, it will be published, the conclave will go on, with or without me. Just let him go, and turn me instead."

"Oh," he says as Abby stirs behind me, "I intend to."

He bites Wyatt anyway. As if for spite, as if for show, as if to punish me, he sinks his fangs into the soft flesh of Wyatt's throat. I can hear the soft, delicate pop as the flesh is punctured and they slice in, ever deeper, as Wyatt squirms and my heart quietly breaks.

The rage boils in me, and now I know how it must feel to hate as the vampires hate.

While Reece gorges on Wyatt's blood, I let the rage wash over me until it blinds the old me and embraces the new. Despite our friendship, I can't see my BFF—only the bloodsucker she's become. I step over Abby, step on Abby, and grab the laptop from the floor. I hold it close against Abby's flesh, searing her throat and left shoulder like a rib eye on a flaming hot grill. She is beyond pain, beyond agony, lying limp among the debris of my broken, ruined phone.

I step into the cage, where Reece is in too much ecstasy over Wyatt's young, fresh, hot blood to see me. Until it's too late.

He looks up, and I smash the laptop into his face, again and again, searing it so close it will take months, maybe years, for his vampire powers to recover. And when his beautiful face is burnt nearly beyond recognition, I keep smashing until the monitor breaks, and I shove the broken shards of glass into and through his smoking, blackened, wizened flesh.

I grab the three flash drives from Reece's smoldering pocket and yank Wyatt off the floor, slinging one of his arms over my shoulder and dragging him out of the cage. I slam the doors shut, sliding the padlock into place as Reece rises, growling, screaming with a rage unlike I've ever witnessed.

# CHAPTER 24

The Mercedes is lightning fast, and it doesn't hurt that I know exactly where I'm going.

*Ralph and Ollie Partied All Night Long.* I repeat it to myself out loud. Wyatt, dazed and confused, rides shotgun. He's sweating profusely, pale, with blood staining the back of his already destroyed T-shirt, while I follow the streets from the warehouse:

Rouse Street.

Andover Lane.

Oliver Street.

Principal Avenue.

Archibald Street.

Ninth Avenue.

Lavender Lane.

*Ralph and Ollie Partied All Night Long.*

I knew it would come in handy!

Once out of the maze Reece drove me through each morning, I hit the main drag and we're back in business. But a long way from being in the clear. Sure, I could keep driving, gun the engine, blow through Beverly Hills, hit the freeway, and just keep going, but then what?

I have the flash drives, I have the code, but . . .

Who will believe me?

They'll think it's all a hoax, some viral stunt to pump up book sales.

I need a better, bigger plan, and it's not out there on the open road. It's here, hitting Reece when he's down, when he's weak.

And I think I have just the place for a final—please let it be final!—showdown.

I cruise through the streets, looking like just another spoiled rich witch in her daddy's Mercedes, taking turns at eighty miles per hour to make sure we have enough time to finish my plan.

Once, in another life, early in my sophomore year when I dated that snowboarder who wound up breaking my heart (or so everybody thinks!), he would often take me to this cheap hotel just inside the 90210 zip code.

Keep your pants on! (I sure did.) We didn't do much. He basically just kept a room there because (a) he was rich enough to afford it, (b) he hated dorm life at Nightshade Academy, and (c) I was the only one who knew about it. OK, sure, we'd make out—and then some—but basically he just played his video games while I munched on corn chips and read fashion magazines I'd bought at the drugstore across the street.

But here's the thing: it was right next door to a church. A working church, the kind with mass and a gift shop and priests on the ground and collection plates and lots and lots of what I need the most right now: blessed, clean, pure holy water.

I know because every time he'd pull into the hotel parking lot in his garish, yellow SUV, we'd pass the church, and he'd say, "How convenient. You can sin at one address and then stumble next door to confess." He must have thought it was hilarious because he said it every single time.

When I squeal into the drugstore parking lot across the street from the Jolly Roger Motel, Wyatt nearly hits his head on the dashboard. "Wuzzuwhodat?" he says, rousing from his prevampire slumber, rubbing his neck, the rims of his eyes red, his mouth dry.

"Just give me two minutes," I say before rushing inside, hoping the thirst won't take him in the 180 seconds I'm gone so that I find him gorging on some homeless person or skateboarder in the parking lot.

I come back three minutes later with Gatorade, Slim Jims, candy bars, and a six-pack of cheap water pistols.

He gorges all the way to the hotel, slurping and munching as if he hasn't eaten in days.

I want to tell him to enjoy it, to warn him it's the last human food he'll eat, ever, that once the transformation starts—in about an hour or so—he'll be food-free for the rest of his afterlife.

But I don't; he's been through so much and still has so far to go. Let him learn on his own.

I stow the Mercedes around the back of the hotel, although I'm sure a slug like Reece will have some kind of tag on the car to find it—and quickly.

In fact, I'm counting on it.

I get a room in the back, in the far corner, if only to make it look like we're actually hiding out. Once we get into the room, I stow Wyatt in the bathtub with his junk food.

"Wuzzawhynowgobyebye?" His lips are slathered in chocolate, and a beef stick pokes out the left side of his mouth like an unlit cigarette.

"Five minutes, Wyatt. That's all I need."

I shut the bathroom door behind me, pull the curtains,

and race to the church gift shop.

I come back ten minutes later—can I help it if I got there just as a midday service got out?—with $30 worth of holy water, about five milk jugs' worth. I sit with Wyatt and empty four of them inside the tub.

I know when he doesn't start sizzling right away that he's not in the grips of it yet, that he's still more human than vampire. I smile to think that, for a little while at least, he'll still be Wyatt—my Wyatt, the Wyatt I fell in love with, the Wyatt I'm still in love with—before he becomes Vampire Wyatt and his first instinct is to look at my throat like a giant Slim Jim!

He winks at me. "Nora, what up? Isn't it a little too soon to be bathing together? I mean, not that I mind or anything, but if that's the case, why are we both still dressed?"

"Relax, player, it's not what you think."

It makes me smile to see that he's at least *somewhat* disappointed.

I make him run the water until our clothes are soaked, then fill all six water pistols with the last of the undiluted holy water.

"Stay here," I order, then walk into the other room and sit in the middle of the cheap table. It breaks under my weight (which in a past life would have really bummed me out but now just makes me grin), and I yank off all four legs, whittling each end to a fine, deadly point with my last drugstore purchase: a four-inch paring knife from the very limited housewares selection.

"Jeez." Wyatt swallows the last of his Gatorade as he watches me from the tub. "Rambo much?"

I smile demurely, wondering if we have enough time before Vampire Armageddon to make out.

Naw, probably not.

We do anyway.

# CHAPTER 25

We stand in the tiny closet, soaking wet.

I have four water pistols hidden strategically around my body, while Wyatt, with only his two track pants pockets, has the rest.

I have strapped the stakes to our chests—two each—with strips of spare bedding I found under the sink. We look like children playing war games in the backyard, tiny and scared, but what else can we do? This is who we are, this is where we are, and this is what we have to do if we're going to survive. Now all we can do is wait.

It doesn't take long.

Wyatt bolts when the hotel room door breaks in.

I yank him back, shushing him with a single quivering finger to my lips.

They tear the room apart, two wounded vampires.

Wyatt starts scratching, tearing at his clothes.

"Stop!" I mouth the word.

But he can't.

Not now. Not when the transformation has finally started.

His clothes start smoking, and he screams, his skin turning

to blisters.

Reece rips the closet door off its hinges and literally tosses it across the room. His face is a wreck; one eye is fused shut, with dried blood and scarred skin closing it completely. The other is staring out from a Halloween mask of cuts and gashes, still smoking from the UV overload.

Wyatt leaps from the closet, tearing at his clothes, yanking off his track pants and leaving on the boxers, tearing off his T-shirt to expose bright pink skin, slightly steaming like he's just stepped out of a Jacuzzi on a cold winter's day.

He's scratching himself when Abby launches at him, claws out, shoulders forward, like a pro linebacker hitting a tackling dummy. (You know, if tackling dummies were hot!)

They slam straight through the wall, landing in the bathroom, where Wyatt has the presence of mind to shove Abby into the diluted holy water filling the bathtub.

She sizzles and shrieks, bucking under him like a patient being electrified for her own good, until Wyatt has a change of heart and drags her out just as quickly as he dumped her in.

She lies on the bathroom floor, her skin bleeding and steaming. She coughs up blood, racked with pain.

"It's Abby!" Wyatt cries, patting her wounds and only making it worse.

"It's *Vampire* Abby!" I shout back as Reece yanks me free of the closet, rips the stakes from the arsenal tied to my chest, tosses them to the ground, and throws me onto the nearest bed.

"Aw," he says, pinning my arms with his knees. "True love, isn't that sweet?"

Wyatt's visible through the door-size hole in the cheap drywall between the main room and the bathroom. He stands, looks at the claws sticking out of his hands, licks the fangs poking out of his upper jaw, a bewildered look in his already yellow eyes. “Nora, what’s happening to me?”

“*He’s* happening to you!” I shout, thrashing in vain to get Reece off me.

Reece only smiles and turns to Wyatt. “Relax, my friend. You’re one of us now.”

“Never!” Wyatt lurches forward, claws and fangs out.

“Oh, no?” Reece arches his neck, poking out his fangs and coming within centimeters of my naked, defenseless throat. “Unless you want her to join you in eternity, young Wyatt, I suggest you—”

I knee him in the groin, shove him off me, and rush to Wyatt through the wide, jagged hole in the wall. We huddle in the bathroom as Reece rises from the cheap carpet in the bedroom.

I aim for the two stakes tied to Wyatt’s chest, grab one with each hand, and step through the door.

Reece shoves me back into the bathroom, his arms still so powerful that if I hadn’t slammed headfirst into Wyatt, I would have surely gone into the next room. Or, at least, parts of me would have.

As it is, I land against Wyatt’s stony flesh, my neck pushing one way, my body pulling another. I’m sore and bruised everywhere and shaking with violence and fear and pain.

Wyatt grabs me, frantically, and turns his back to Reece.

I am trapped between my vampire kind-of boyfriend and the bathroom wall, nowhere to go as Reece claws at Wyatt’s back, tearing at bare skin. Blood pools on the bathroom floor.

“Wyatt!” I shout as Reece pulls him slowly back, back toward the hole in the door.

“Nora!” he shouts, fear bringing his fangs forward to full

point, nearly four inches of hungry, trembling fangs mere centimeters from my face.

I see my future in those long, sharp teeth: I see Reece tearing at him, eventually yanking him away and finding me—and then turning me. There is no avoiding it. There is no way out but this. This isn't one of the scenes in my stupid books, and I'm no Scarlet Stain. I can't break his arm with a karate chop or rig the shower curtain into a parachute and fly away from this one.

This is real life, strange as it all may be, and here is where this life—my life—must end.

Reece is too strong. Even with a face full of laptop glass and UV rays, even wounded and weakened, he is tearing Wyatt to bits.

The only way to stop it is to sacrifice myself.

To release my bond to humanity, to become . . . immortal.

I grab Wyatt, embracing him, once again bringing his head to my neck, like that day in the commons at school.

It seems so long ago, yet I know it wasn't.

But it was a simpler, more innocent time. He was human then, warm and soft and tender to the touch, his lips so warm and fang-free, his tongue so eager, his hands so firm and self-assured as they pulled me toward him like he'd done it a thousand times before—like he was a pro, taking control, calling the shots.

But now it's my turn to take control, to call the shots, to pull him close, ever closer, to me. Not as a ruse to fool Bianca this time, but for the real deal.

"Nora!" he shouts, too weak from blood loss to resist.

Before Reece can yank him away, before I can chicken out, I jam his fangs into my throat like a can opener, plunging them deeper, deeper, into the skin, past the skin, until I can literally feel the connection between us, between his teeth and my jugular, the biggest, fattest, most powerful vein in the human body.

It breaks like a sewer main, spewing blood into those fangs like that gum with the soft, squishy, squirty middle, his vampire venom mixing with mine.

The sensation is immediate, the power immense, the rush incredible.

I can feel our DNA fusing, my humanity drifting, my blood pumping, nearly boiling with the power, the fear, of immortality.

And I'm so glad, no matter what happens next, that it's Wyatt who turns me and not Reece.

Or Bianca.

Or even Abby.

I don't pass out so much as slump.

Down the dirty tiles of the bathroom wall, down onto the wet floor, which vaguely sizzles against my bare ankles in a not entirely unpleasant way.

Wyatt still stands, wiping the blood—my blood—from his lips.

As if he's embarrassed, as if he's ashamed, of what he's done. Scratch that—of what I've done.

Reece immediately stops his assault on Wyatt's back and squeezes through the hole in the crumbling drywall to see for himself if I've really done what he thinks I've done. I don't disappoint.

Standing calmly next to Wyatt—as if 2.7 seconds earlier he wasn't trying to claw his way to his spinal cord—Reece looks down almost wistfully. "It's a shame, really. I was looking forward to tasting her myself."

He slaps Wyatt on his torn back. "Ah well, young man, to the victor go the spoils, eh?"

"Now what?" Wyatt pulls a dry towel from a rack on the dirty yellow wall and wraps his snacks in it. He's bathed in a halo of red light as my human sight gives way to creepy vampire vision.

"Now we leave this place and destroy the evidence," Reece says.

"What evidence?" Wyatt looks down at Abby's steaming body.

"That," Reece says, and the way he says it lets me know I'll always hate him, until the day I die—again.

Or he does.

Whichever comes first.

# CHAPTER 26

"Hold on, *hold* on, hold *on*," I snap from my inglorious seat on the wet bathroom floor. I stand and shove them both away from Abby's body with a strength I never knew I could possess. "This isn't evidence; this is my friend. This is my *best* friend."

Wyatt says, "Nora, she's tried to kill you, by my count, like six times today alone. And she literally just tried to break me in half. What do you think she's going to do tomorrow? And the next day?"

I stand over her, nonplussed. "That was when I was human, Wyatt. And if you'd turned a little earlier, you probably would have done the same thing."

He shakes his head, his unsightly red skin already healing from the holy water bathtub trip.

I look at Abby lying on the floor, her face a mass of boils, her hair choppy and short where half of it has burned away (oh, she's gonna kill me—if she lives, that is), her shoulder a red, ghastly thing, her clothes tattered, the skin underneath covered in welts.

"The only reason she's lying here in the first place is because *you* pulled her out of that tub, Wyatt. Remember that? You've already saved her once today. Now you want to get rid of her like some piece of trash all of a sudden? What's gotten *into* you?"

He rubs his head, shakes it, like he can't believe what I'm suggesting. His eyes are full of wonder, then pain, then shame, then anger, then . . . confusion. (Hey, I know the feeling!)

"I can't believe you, Wyatt. This was your girlfriend once upon a time! You two were intimate. Remember? Think about it—is this really someone you want to do away with? Forever?"

He clings to the shredded bathroom wall, grout and concrete dust turning to mud on his long fingers. He seems unable, maybe even unwilling, to look at Abby.

Reece says nothing, merely watches our sad little drama unfold as I kneel on the floor to touch Abby's cheek.

It is hot, no doubt, but alive.

And as I watch, I can see the skin starting to heal, to grow less pink, the boils no longer pulsing now.

I put my finger beneath her bent nose. She's still breathing. I snap my finger next to her ear, and she flinches, just the tiniest bit—just enough to let me know she's still in there somewhere.

"We can't let her die like this," I insist. "Isn't there anything we can do?"

Reece looks at me curiously. Just then sirens wail, and his panicked face takes on an almost feral look. "It's too late now anyway." He seems almost disappointed we won't be disposing of anybody anymore. "Grab her, Wyatt, and both of you follow me. Quickly now. I'm tired of fighting and don't wish to take on the entire Beverly Hills police force if I can avoid it."

As Wyatt reluctantly picks up Abby and slings her over

his shoulder like a big, red, steaming duffel bag, I reach for one of the water pistols in my pocket.

Reece leads us out of the room, down the stairs, and straight to his car. Even with a trio of half-vampires straggling behind him and sirens blaring just down the street, Reece has the presence of mind to turn to me and slap the gun out of my hand with one effortless, perfectly aimed swipe. "Where we're going," he says ominously over his shoulder, "you'll want me around. Trust me. I know you don't believe it now, but you will once we get there."

"Where are we *going* anyway?" I ask fifteen minutes later, once the coast is clear and we're barreling down the 101 heading west.

I'm riding shotgun, strapped into the seat so tightly I couldn't go anywhere even if I wanted to.

My body feels leaden, each muscle sore.

Wyatt is directly behind me, enduring his own hellish transformation, with Abby just behind Reece, beyond pain, beyond consciousness—partway between human and what she is—what we all are—destined to become.

The sleek sports car with the black-tinted windows roars down the freeway, deserted at this time of night, speeds reaching ninety, sometimes one hundred miles per hour as we race toward parts unknown.

"She needs expert help if she's to heal properly," he explains as if we're a nuisance and he'd rather just keep driving. "The kind of help only the Council of Ancients can provide."

"I know I'm a little out of it," I croak, barely finding the strength to speak, "but did you just say . . . Council of *Ancients*? You mean, they really *do* exist?"

"Of course they do," he snaps impatiently (I realize this is his default setting, not sure how I ever missed that before), changing lanes to fly past an eighteen-wheeler going too slow in the right-hand lane—at eighty-seven miles per hour. "You didn't get entirely *everything* wrong in those silly books of yours."

"But why are you taking us there?" I ask, ignoring his blatant cut down. (Trust me, I've heard worse.)

He sighs, hand steady on the wheel as my eyes flutter open and shut intermittently, completely out of my control.

It's like I've been awake for seventy-two hours straight and am starting to zone out without rhyme or reason. Then I realize it must be the vampire in me, short-circuiting everything I've ever known.

"Believe it or not, Nora," Reece says, not without some obvious discomfort, "you are not the *only* one at fault in this whole mess. I too have sinned: sinned against my tribe, my kind, and the laws set down by the Ancients themselves."

"You?" Wyatt says from the backseat, a wary look on his face. "The great and mighty Reece Rothchild screwed up? How so?"

"You, actually," he says to Wyatt, giving him a vicious case of side-eye in the rearview mirror. "It has been forbidden since the great Overabundance Act of 1990 to turn any new males into vampires. There are simply too many of us as it is. By turning you, I too have sinned. I too must face the wrath of the Ancients."

"You *too*?" I sputter. I am fading fast but still managing to grasp the logic of what he's laying down. "Who *else* sinned?"

"Why, you, Nora, of course," he says, as if it gives him great comfort to deliver the news that I've been a very bad girl. "*You* broke the code, *you* threatened to publish it to the world, and what's worse, *you* killed one of your own."

"Killed? Who'd I kill?" I'm an author, for Pete's sake; I've never hurt another living soul, let alone killed a person, in my entire life.

"Have you already forgotten about poor Bianca and that desk leg you shoved through her heart back in the warehouse?"

"That was *before*! I was human then. I was a mortal who could die, and she *knew* that. Plus, your beloved girlfriend was trying to kill *me*! Have you already forgotten that darling little detail? Poor Bianca, my left foot!"

Reece gives me that famous smile. "That's not the way I'll be telling it to the Ancients."

"You *creep*!" Wyatt shouts from the backseat, weakly kicking the polished leather Reece is sitting on. "I saw the whole thing. Bianca was trying to kill Nora; Nora was human then, and she was just trying to defend herself."

"You?" Reece sneers, as if he has something unpleasant on his shoe he can't get off. "You're hardly what I'd call a reliable witness, dear boy. You were barely conscious at the time, you blithering fool. It's bad enough I have to suffer for my sin. I'm not going to suffer alone. The harder they punish Nora, the less likely they'll be to punish me."

Wyatt fusses a little longer, I'll give him that, but by this point I've all but given up.

I don't care what happens to Reece; I can't believe I ever did.

Heck, right about now I don't even care what happens to *me*.

I feel . . . not good.

It's like an instant flu bug, gone straight to my head, my throat . . . my heart.

Something is happening inside me—something uncontrollable, wild, and angry.

One second I'm short of breath, gasping for air; the next I'm relaxed and euphoric, absolutely high; then it's right back to some kind of panic attack for my lungs.

I feel nauseated, sore, lightheaded, and . . . amazing?

I'm smiling even as tears roll down my face, flinching as elation floods my body, quivering from head to toe as I bliss out in the buttery leather of the seat beneath me.

It's the purest definition of bittersweet, this leaving my old me behind and embracing the new.

"I never *did* like you," I murmur, succumbing to the agony, the ecstasy, the pain, and the delight as they consume me all at once.

"The feeling's more than mutual, Nora, but say no more. We have several hours to travel before we arrive at the Council of Ancients. That should be just enough time for you to turn completely and accept—"

There is more, but the exhaustion has finally overtaken me. Gladly, I succumb to my body's need for sleep, never regretting for one second that I won't get to hear the end of another one of Reece's grand soliloquies . . .

# CHAPTER 27

I awake to the sound of tires crunching on gravel and light so strong it seems to be pouring through the heavy tint of Reece's Mercedes windows and piercing my very skull. I blink, raising my hands against the sun's blinding rays, and someone hands me a pair of thick, wraparound sunglasses from the glove box.

"Here," Reece says with little emotion, "these will help protect you."

"Protect me from *what*?"

"Your new eyesight," he says impatiently, and I notice we are on a back road now, surrounded by trees.

I slide on the sunglasses and feel instant relief.

"Is it daylight already?" I ask rhetorically.

"No," he answers quietly, and with my normal vision restored by the sunglasses, I can see we're on another deserted stretch of open highway. "But vampires can see in the dark, so at night it will be bright like it's daytime. Welcome to the fold, Nora."

It's so amazing to me that the dark could feel so light. I

can't help but wonder what the light will feel like when the sun finally does rise. "Ugh, don't remind me."

He smiles, and for the briefest moment I can put behind me the horrible things he's done—the wretched things he's made *me* do—and see the handsome young man who showed up at my book signing that fateful night only a few days ago.

The plunge back into my past makes the hard, blunt edges of my reality all the more difficult to focus on.

If only I could go back and start over. If only I could ignore Reece's chocolate-brown eyes, his chiseled cheekbones, his graceful style, but then . . . what? He still would have gotten to me and seduced me or at least tricked me into writing the book for him.

I was played, straight up-and-down dirty, and the shame burns more because I leaped so willingly into his little scheme.

"You of all people should be grateful," he's saying, his speech only slightly slurred through the ravages of his half-seared face. "Now you can truly write from a vampire's perspective."

"That's rich." I snort. "Have you even *read* one of my books? I mean, not just to trick me into thinking you have, but . . . all the way through?"

He shrugs, easing the car up past ninety miles per hour as the grade in the road levels out.

I know California is hilly and wonder exactly where we are.

The night is so dark, the road so barren, the sky so empty, we could be anywhere: north, south, east, west.

We could have been driving around in circles all this time, for all I know, or headed to Canada or Texas!

"God no," he says in answer to my question. "I could

barely get through one chapter before I had enough. Why?"

"Because if you ever bothered to read one of my books, you would know that my main character, Scarlet Stain, *isn't* a vampire. She's a vampire hunter. Duh!"

"Well, maybe now you'll have a little more sympathy for your villain. What's his name? Count Fichus? Count Rictus?"

"Count *Victus*," I correct, looking out the window to see yet another patch of identical roadside emptiness fly past the heavily tinted windows. "Where are we, anyway?"

"Almost there," he answers without answering, a specialty of his. "Almost there."

As he concentrates on the driving, I look behind me to see Wyatt, sleeping, still clutching the cheap bath towel from the motel room. While it is saturated through with deep-red blood, his skin looks mostly healed. In fact, I'd say he looks better than ever. The slight smile on his face, the upturned lips, and healthy glow of his olive skin suggest he's experiencing that same bittersweet bliss I felt before napping out. I can't see his back, but as he sleeps, he doesn't seem to be in any noticeable pain. His color is back, his flesh alive, his breathing regular.

Passed out next to him and looking *really* uncomfortable strapped into the backseat, Abby is not so lucky. Although her skin looks less red now, her breathing is still shallow, her skin mottled, her clothes tattered and revealing large scars that look like they'll never go away.

I turn back around in my seat and watch the mountains rise in front of us. Reece is focusing intently on the road ahead, his face a mask of pain and regret tinged with that smirk of confidence he just can't seem to wipe away, regardless of the dire circumstances we both seem to be in.

"How do you feel?"

Is that the faintest trace of . . . concern I hear in his voice? Probably not, but still. At this point I'll take whatever I can get.

I should feel awful. I mean, I'm a vampire, right? But I actually feel . . . great. Like I've just slept for the entire weekend and gotten up three hours before my alarm goes off on Monday morning, ready to run a 5K before homeroom.

I open my mouth to complain but can't. "Pretty good," I admit, the faintest trace of a smile at the corner of my lips.

"See what you've been missing all this time?" he asks knowingly, his grip firm on the wheel as we continue to speed across the country toward God knows where to greet God knows what.

"That remains to be seen." I sigh.

"Oh, I think you'll be surprised by the world that awaits you. *If* the Ancients let you live, of course."

His words echo through the car, sober and severe. "One last step before your transformation is complete."

Then he lightly taps the leather armrest between us, and it hisses open on state-of-the-art hydraulics.

Attached to the upper panel are several IV bags full of what looks like rich, thick *blood.*

"I'm a little occupied," he says. "Help yourself."

I grab a bag, the metal clip clicking off the hanging rack like a bag of chips in a vending machine. There is a straw affixed to the bag, like a giant vampire juice box, just the thing for those late-night picnics.

"Like this?" I ask, taking off the silver seal of the straw.

He doesn't bother glancing over.

"I'm not your *father,*" he says a tad viciously, that nasty streak bubbling to the surface again. "What will you do when I'm not around to protect you?"

I shrug. "Kick up my heels?" I wrap my mouth around the straw and give it a good—

Whoa, this is some grade-A, primo refreshment here!

I suck ravenously, the dense liquid seeming to evaporate in a blissful taste sensation the minute it hits my tongue. I feel a vague pressure in my upper jaw, like the first few minutes at the dentist's office when he's probing your teeth with that little pick. Reaching up to my mouth, I feel my fangs protruding.

I can't believe this is actually happening.

I.

Have.

Frickin'.

Fangs!

The blood doesn't fill me up so much as . . . satisfy me.

I can't feel anything in my stomach, but I'm full and my thirst has been quenched.

Completely. Absolutely.

Still I reach for another bag and drain it dry, the life source flowing through me like water down a theme park flume ride, gushing into my dry cells, plumping them up, fleshing them out, making them—making me—feel suddenly complete.

Only when I reach for the third bag does Reece say, "Save some for your friends! God, there's nothing worse than a greedy vampire. Well, except for a *new* greedy vampire, I suppose."

I pull my hand back guiltily, like the party guest caught reaching for the last cupcake. The hydraulic gears maneuver the leather armrest back into place until it looks like, well, just another $3,000 imported car armrest.

"Nifty," I say. "Even James Bond doesn't have one of those."

"I'd kick Bond's *butt*," Reece says, a cocky grin playing against his half fangs.

I chuckle, blood-buzzed and in a forgiving mood. "We'll just have to see about that—"

# CHAPTER 28

Blinding lights cut me off midsentence, jarring me even through the heavy coating on my new sunglasses. I wince and instinctively shrink back from the lights, scrambling to pull as far away as I can, but my ultrasafety seat belt snags and keeps me in place. I sit there and stare, unblinking, a deer frozen in the headlights.

Reece hits the brakes immediately, plunging all of us forward against our seat belts. The sound of our clattering teeth is almost as loud as his squealing tires on the empty pavement. The car doesn't stop instantly, like it might in a movie or some pricey sports car commercial, but instead fishtails awkwardly, the heavy back end coming around to meet the front as we slide sideways. The oncoming lights shine straight into my eyes.

Still we slide, the rush of momentum carrying us forward haphazardly until my door panel crashes into the bright lights, shutting them off and sealing me in with a gasping crunch. Metal slams on metal as the door bends inward, the interior of Reece's car melting like butter.

Our engine races in place, revving faster and faster until

I think Reece might still have his foot plastered against the gas pedal. Then suddenly the car shudders before the motor stalls completely with a staggering, swaggering sigh of hissing steam and gushing radiator fluid.

In the silence that follows, I hear glass tinkling on the deserted roadway, then doors opening, then heavy footsteps grinding glass into dust.

Reece hisses next to me, his face a mask of pain—or, at least, annoyance—and I see the steering wheel sticking into his rib cage. He pulls it off like I've seen Wyatt pull off a wet tank top, then tosses it on the dashboard with a resounding clank. He stretches, peeling back his shirt to reveal a dent the size of the steering wheel in his chest. In moments it shimmers and gels until his chest is solid and seamless again.

There is groaning from the back as Wyatt comes to life, his face a mask of pain. I look down and see why—the back door is bent inward and pressing against his thigh.

Abby's eyelids flutter. Her neck is bent at an odd angle, but she's still unconscious. As activity blurs all around me—a dozen or more pairs of shoes crunching on the empty highway surrounding our car—I idly wonder if she isn't the lucky one right about now.

Reece looks at me, and I'm thinking he's concerned, but then my blurry eyes focus and it's clear he's looking straight past me, out my shattered window. I follow his line of vision and see several large, black vans, with two or three hulking figures at a time pouring out the side doors. It's like watching giant ants scatter out of a broken ant farm—only they're in control and we're the ones who are broken. Because they're the ones who broke us.

Whoever *they* are.

Reece spits blood onto the dashboard, thick like Jell-O that's been left on the kitchen counter too long.

I watch it ooze into the air-conditioning vents until he curses, "Guardians!"

"Huh?"

Dark shapes filter past our headlights as I gaze weakly into the distance.

"Guardians, Nora. The ones I warned you about. Like vampire cops. Here to take us to their leaders."

"Who would be—?"

"Why, the Council of Ancients, my dear."

Black uniforms, ghostly white faces, shaved heads, and vicious yellow fangs clamor for entrance into Reece's luxury sedan.

I sputter, "Those don't look like any cops I've ever seen bef—"

Suddenly Reece's door is yanked off its hinges, a thousand pounds of metal tossed aside like some giant Frisbee—with cup holders.

I hear it crash onto the street several yards away and wince as it scrapes against the lonely blacktop, shuttling off sparks until it slides to a stop another dozen yards past the chunk of road where it landed.

Reece doesn't struggle, doesn't fight, merely glances at the gigantic bald head looming into his doorway—*filling* his doorway—and grins. "Hi, fellas! What took you so long?"

The bald guy—a Guardian? *The* Guardian? I can't tell 'cause everyone's ignoring me, which is probably a *good* thing—grabs Reece and drags him from the front seat, torn seat belt and all.

Headlights suddenly turn into spotlights, as the Guardian

stands Reece up on the road only to punch him, several times, in the gut. Hard. Like action-movie hard; like he-wouldn't-survive-it-if-he-weren't-already-undead hard.

Reece spits up more blood, and from the backseat I hear, "About damn time somebody kicked that creep's butt!" Wyatt unclicks his seat belt and scoots over to check on Abby's less-than-vital vital signs.

"It's not him I'm worried about," I whisper.

The Guardian leans Reece onto the hood and whips out a gleaming hypodermic needle from one of the many pockets in his black uniform, then shoves it into his neck.

"What's bothering me is what they're going to do when they get tired of playing with him."

# CHAPTER 29

I come to in somebody's cellar. At least, that's what it looks like.

Water is dripping somewhere, naturally, because when you wake up in a cellar, there is *always* water dripping somewhere.

My head feels slightly fuzzy, like it does when I wake up after taking one too many cold pills.

I sit upright and rub my forehead, finding it grimy, but hey, at least my hands aren't bound.

I blink, glad for my newfound vampire vision as the details of my cell become clearer.

The walls are slick with some kind of runoff, but they're tiled and white and not exactly cellar-ish, if you know what I mean.

More like some kind of old hospital waiting room or something.

I am alone, propped up in a corner, which would explain the crick in my neck and the ache at the base of my spine.

I stand, surprised my legs have not been bound either.

I soon find out why: the double doors to the room are locked.

I rattle them, shake them, try to yank them open—and off—the way the giant Guardian did with Reece's door, but I guess I'm not that kind of a vampire yet.

I stalk the room, stretching my legs, arching my sore arms over my head, tilting my head from side to side like I used to do after a long night hunched over the keyboard writing about Count Victus.

The floor is clean cement, and a few scattered chairs are stacked in one odd corner. I look at them, smiling faintly because they look just like the blue-and-orange chairs they used in Nightshade's cafeteria.

The room is quiet, but the hallway outside is bustling, and I wonder how long it will be before the Guardians come and collect me for whatever it is they've hijacked us for.

I stand looking at the stack of chairs, feeling the vague sting in my neck from the needle the Guardian shoved in just after tearing off my own car door and peering in with his leering, fanged smile.

Now here I am, somewhere, alone in a room, water dripping and footsteps marching in my direction.

I grab the top chair and lift it off, fairly effortlessly. It is molded blue plastic, fixed to four metal legs. There are really only two metal legs, though; each has been bent in the middle to create two legs.

The footsteps stop outside my door.

I whimper vaguely, if only to cover the sound of me prying the thin blue plastic off the double chair legs. It yields surprisingly easily, not much more difficult than peeling the stubborn lid off a tub of margarine.

I smile, wondering how long that would have taken me last week, when I was still a mortal.

I toss the plastic seat in a far corner and yank the two legs apart. I'm left with one leg, long and metal and shaped kind of like an upside-down *U*. I straighten it in the middle, like a pipe cleaner in kindergarten craft time, until it is one long leg about the size of your average sword.

I hide it behind my back, tiptoeing toward the middle of the room, as keys clatter in the lock of my double doors.

A Guardian appears, his head gleaming in the weak overhead lighting of my sad little hospital room. He's at least a foot taller than I am, and his face is expressionless as he inches in.

I think, *This isn't going to be so hard, after all.* I tense my hands on the bar at my back. I'm ready to pull it out and go all samurai on that shiny chrome dome, when in walks another Guardian, then two more.

I creep back; they creep forward.

Soon Guardians fill the small room, and I sigh, letting the metal bar clang to the floor.

The one in front breaks rank and oozes a small, weak smile before zipping it back up. "Nora Falcon?" he asks.

I look around with a snarky *Who, me?* face.

He's not having it.

"Nora Falcon," he says louder.

I nod.

Nodding back, he barks, "Come with us."

I shrug and take a step toward him. "Promise you won't drug me this time," I say as the hulks surround me and lead me from the room.

"That was for your protection," says the big lug who asked my name.

"Really? What exactly does knocking me out cold and locking me up in some deranged hospital room have to do with my protection?"

He grunts. "The less you know about our location, the better."

I follow silently, suddenly wondering if this is where Reece was taking us all along: the Council of Ancients.

The hallway is long and wide, as if it were built big enough to accommodate golf carts—or tanks.

Lights flicker overhead as we pass door after door. We don't turn; we just walk straight and fast, and the hallway seems to go on forever.

The pack of Guardians separates from us a little as we walk. Some slow down; some speed up. They don't quite leave, but they're not tripping all over me anymore either. Eventually it's me and the Big Guy.

"Where are you taking me?"

Without looking down at me, he says, "The Council is very eager to see you, Nora Falcon."

I grin to hear him say both of my names like that: Nora Falcon. Like he's some alien from another planet and thinks you always say both names, every time, even after you've been formally introduced.

"What about Reece?"

He doesn't answer right away.

Oh yeah, I forgot. "What about Reece *Rothchild*?"

Big Guy stutter-steps just for a second, then grunts. "The Council is even *more* eager to see him." There is something so menacing in his tone, it makes me think the Ancients aren't the only ones around here eager to see Reece.

"Yeah, I heard about all that. I mean . . . where is he? Has he come? And gone? Do I have to see him again?"

Big Guy starts to answer. I can see the muscles on the back of his neck as his jaw opens, but suddenly we turn one last corner, and my answer is there, waiting for me.

"Hello, Nora. Have a nice sleep?"

# CHAPTER 30

Reece looks rumpled but rested.

"Where'd you get the snazzy clothes?" I ask, noticing his all-white ensemble. Somewhere along the line he lost his last outfit, stained as it was with his own skin. Now he looks pretty radiant, the starched white linen clinging to his lean, muscular body, even if the high collar of his shirt highlights the dark red of his melted, seared, goopy face. He looks back at me with a quizzical smile. "Same place you got yours, sunshine. Courtesy of our good friends, the Guardians, here."

I look down and, sure enough, I'm in the same clothes, covered from head to toe in white linen—and nothing else. The material is loose but comfortable, and on my feet are soft slippers, the kind with backs. Reece has them on too. Suddenly self-conscious, I blush to think who changed me, how long it took, where my other clothes went—and why.

I feel my hair; it's damp. I smell my wrist, and there is the slight scent of cheap, generic, public school sink soap lingering on my pale skin. You mean . . . they bathed me too?

Naturally, Reece is enjoying my suffering. He opens his blistered mouth—

But Big Guy cuts him off. "We had to make you presentable for the Ancients, Nora. Don't worry; you were attended to by a female."

"You mean there are female Guardians?" I look around the crowded vestibule area to see some long, flowing—maybe even red—tresses among the shimmering, identical bald heads.

Reece laughs triumphantly and says, "Not bloody likely, Nora. There hasn't been a female Guardian in centuries."

"Well, that doesn't sound fair."

Reece merely snorts.

We are standing in a waiting room of sorts, the kind you'd see outside a courtroom, with empty bulletin boards on the wall and benches beneath.

Reece sits on one; the rest are empty.

The Guardians stand around, erect and silent but occasionally shifting their weight nervously.

I gulp. These Ancient dudes must be pretty badass to make the Guardians nervous.

Reece is admiring me coolly, sitting back on the bench, arms open wide across the back of it, legs crossed daintily.

I ask him, "What happened out there?"

He shrugs. "An ambush, no doubt. It was bound to happen, I suppose."

"But why? You were taking us to the Ancients anyway, so why did—?"

Big Guy chuckles, which is a first. "Taking you *here*? Is that what he told you? Nora Falcon, he was running away, headed in the opposite direction."

"What?"

Despite all that happened, how many times he fooled me

already, it never occurred to me that Reece would try to run from the Ancients.

But then . . . maybe he had a very good reason.

"Running?" He smirks jauntily, as if Big Guy isn't strong enough to break him in two like a toothpick after a very large dinner. "Who said I was running? Just taking a little detour; that's all."

I look at Big Guy and say, "Forget him. What about my friends?" My voice is slightly hysterical now, my blood boiling to think I might get blamed for Reece's stupid high jinks.

Reece says, "They're fine, Nora—"

Big Guy silences him with a wave. "They are being healed," he says quietly, giving me a wise but gentle glance.

I start to open my mouth, but the big double doors crack open slightly, and the Big Guy quiets me with the hardest case of side-eye I've ever seen. "The Ancients will see you now," he says grimly.

Even Reece rises without cockiness, without comment, without so much as a sneer.

# CHAPTER 31

Seven Ancients sit along a far wall on a long couch.

This room is like the one I woke up in, only about four thousand times bigger. White tiles line the wall, thousands of them, hundreds of thousands of them. Millions, maybe. But unlike in my tiny waiting room, these are clean and bleached white and stretch two, three, maybe four stories high.

The couch is low but looks soft, like something you might find in a very, very rich person's house.

Unlike the modern room, the Ancients look frail and impossibly old. Their hair is either gone completely or silky white and sparse, their skin so paper thin and pale you can almost see through it to the fat, black vampire veins pulsing just beneath. Their eyes are shrunken and opaque; they might all have cataracts, like my grandmother in the nursing home back in Florida. Some of their fangs are permanently out now, like those sports cars with pop-up headlights that after a while never go back down; they are yellowed by time and, perhaps, use. Some fangs are gnarled and broken, others so thin and sharp they're more like needles than teeth.

They are dressed all in white—white linen, to be precise, just like the material Reece and I are dressed in. Well, at least, in *theory.* On the Ancients it hangs like big brother's hand-me-downs on a third grader: drawstring pants, pirate-type shirts with ties at the neck and puffy sleeves around bony wrists, white slip-on shoes like your grandfather might wear to shuffle around the porch yelling at stray cats that aren't there and haven't been for six years.

They sit in a row, close enough to lean against one another should their hearts suddenly give out but far enough away for me to realize that the couch is in fact seven high, padded chairs pushed together.

Next to each Ancient is a cane with a silver tip, and behind each puffy white chair a black-clad Guardian stands at the ready, uniform stiff, spine stiffer, with gleaming, shaved heads like white cherries on top of an evil sundae.

Two smaller chairs are lined up next to each other facing the Ancients at a great distance away.

Four Guardians, their legs long, their arms bulging with sculpted muscles, their faces blank masks of endless rage, show us into the Council's giant meeting room and guide us efficiently to our seats.

They remain guarding us long after Reece and I sit down.

The giant room is deathly quiet.

The Ancients shift slowly in their seats, some crossing their legs, some clacking their jaws, some combing clawed fingers through wispy hair. In the awkward silence that fills the room, I try to picture where we might be and why the Ancients have chosen this place.

I feel disoriented, not knowing how we got here or how far it is from the accident in the middle of that deserted road or even, for that matter, what the outside of this building looks like. Is the entrance old and decrepit like my waiting room? Or clean and modern like this gargantuan meeting hall?

Are we high atop a mountain or far underground?

Heck, for all I know, we could be underwater. I haven't seen a window since I woke up.

The room, the hallways, the white linen, the sparkling tile, the vaguely antiseptic smell that lingers everywhere—all give the place a scientific feel, like maybe we're in the bowels of some giant laboratory. Rats in a maze. The imagery seems fitting, though I don't dare say that out loud.

No one speaks for quite some time.

Reece is uncharacteristically quiet. He sits erect, his face a mask. I know he's angry, I'm sure he feels this gathering is beneath him, but I also know he must sit here just like me and take his punishment.

Oh, how it must kill him to do so, especially since he was running away when the Guardians tracked us down and found us.

What will his penalty be for that, I wonder, on top of all the other crimes—or are they sins—he's already committed?

He focuses directly ahead. Even when I peek at him, he stares straight at some point over the Ancients' heads.

Time passes. Who knows how much? One hour, two . . . three? I get the feeling that for vampires this old, time isn't quite the same as it is for a busy teenage author.

I hear no clock ticking, no feet moving, no water dripping; only the steady flickering of endless rows of dense overhead fluorescent lighting and the ceaseless pounding of my cold and undead heart.

Finally, a firm voice issues from the Ancient sitting in the middle of his dusty, moldy comrades. "Reece," the voice says much clearer—and louder—than I imagined. "Kneel before the Ancients to plead your case."

"Master," Reece says, his voice suddenly gentle and oddly reverent. He quickly stands, then just as quickly kneels. "I come here today with great sorrow in my heart, for I readily confess that I have broken one of the Ancient laws."

"Which law didst thou break?" asks another Ancient from the end of the row of seven, his lips barely moving.

"Our most recent, Your Lordship. I confess to turning a mortal male into one of us."

There is no gasp, no sound of shock or outrage, just a quiet murmuring among the pale faces that make up the Council of Ancients. They don't even look at one another; it appears they've been together so long, they no longer need to.

A clear voice interrupts the murmuring: "May I ask, Reece, what happened to your face?"

Reece shoots me a look. His scarred eye is still sealed shut by rough, red tissue. "I was attacked, my lord," he explains through gritted teeth, embarrassment and anger leaking through his otherwise solemn speech.

"By one of us?" asks the Ancient in the middle, his voice so smooth you could pour it out of a crystal decanter into a waiting rocks glass and serve it to an ambassador at high tea.

"Unfortunately, no, my lord. By a . . . mortal."

The word seems to offend his tongue—and everyone in the room.

A ripple passes through the Ancients, some mumbling, others looking to their left, their right, as if to confirm that what they've heard—a mortal wounded a vampire?—is more than a fairy tale.

I am offended at their offense, until I remember: I'm no longer mortal, so why should I care?

The Ancient in the middle looks at me for the first time, his eyes so alive and yellow I can't look away.

"By *this* mortal?" he asks, somewhat surprised, although he sounds more impressed than disappointed.

"She is, alas, no longer mortal," Reece says. "But yes, she is the one who attacked me."

At this the Ancients smile to themselves, so briefly I wouldn't have even noticed it if I hadn't been transfixed by their almost lipless smiles.

"I see," says one, no amusement in his hollow voice.

Beside me, so close I could reach out and push him over—and I'm sorely tempted but for the Big Guy Guardian behind me who'll shoot me full of holes the instant I flinch—Reece literally trembles in the face of these seven tiny, wizened men.

"Reece, rise and accept your fate," says the Ancient in the middle of the group. I wish these guys wore nametags so I could call them something other than *the Ancient in the middle.*

Reece stands slowly, as if taking his time will further delay his sentence or, perhaps, prevent it. Eventually he's at his full height, and even now I am startled by how big he is.

To think I tussled with a vampire of his stature, of his experience, of his ferocity, and lived to tell the tale impresses me. To think that I wounded him, however insignificantly, blows me away. Take that, you pretty-boy, smooth-talking, code-planting, running-away-from-the-Ancients creep!

"Reece," says the Ancient in the middle, "for breaking one of the Sacred Laws, for turning a male into a vampire, we sentence you to . . . a life of scars. You will not be fully cured by the powers of our ancient Healers. Instead you will suffer your fate in silence, never to speak of it nor try to remedy it. Every day, when people look upon your face in horror, when even vampires are shocked and sickened at the mere sight of you, you will be reminded of your transgressions. And you will be humbled by the power of this Council over your fate."

"But, my lord," Reece says, forgetting all former propriety, "how am I to accomplish my work of seducing mortals with . . . with . . . *this*? Surely you must allow me some comfort from my hideous countenance!" He points to his face, withered and scarred, eye permanently shut and half of his formerly dazzling smile disfigured.

I see his point.

Secretly, I smile at his suffering.

"You should have thought of that, Reece," one of the Ancients says, "before you broke our Laws."

And still he argues, voice getting louder, more indignant with each word. "But it was a crime of passion, a momentary lapse of—"

"Silence," screams the Ancient in the middle as he rises effortlessly from his chair and literally sails across the room, his little feet barely touching the floor as he covers the vast space of this gargantuan room blindingly fast.

He lands in front of Reece with barely a whisper and grabs his neck. His pale hands are soon digging into Reece's supple flesh with a power that shocks even Reece. "Do you dare to question the authority of the *Ancients*?" he asks, voice barely above a whisper.

Reece flinches, eyes filled with dread, barely able to choke out a gurgled, "N-n-no, my lord," through the Ancient's iron grip around his Adam's apple.

But the Ancient isn't through with him yet. Still clutching

Reece's throat, the withered but powerful vampire says, "You are lucky we allow you to *exist,* Reece. This isn't your first . . . How did you put it? Oh, yes: *lapse of reason.* And am I to understand that on top of all the crimes committed on this assignment, when the Guardians found you, you were running away from your appointed meeting with us?

"For shame, Reece. For shame. Even for you, that news is shocking and disappointing. Perhaps now you will remember why you are being disciplined, in order to avoid further punishment. *Permanent* punishment. Or have you forgotten, or perhaps chosen to ignore, the power of this Council before which you kneel today?" Then the Ancient releases his grip.

Reece falls to the ground in a big, pale heap that continues trembling long after his ignoble fall from grace. I glance briefly at his neck, only to see bright red welts in the shape of deep, flaming fingerprints. For some reason—shoot, for many reasons—the sight is supremely satisfying.

Two Guardians pull him away, the sound of his boots dragging down the endless hallway. The only thing louder is the groan of his disappointment echoing off the high, thick walls.

When at last the double doors at the end of the hall open and close and silence once again fills the room, the Ancient who strangled Reece looks at me with an expression of curiosity bordering on contempt. I wish he'd fly back across the room where he can lecture me from a safe distance, but instead he comes even closer.

It takes every ounce of willpower I have not to scramble deeper and deeper into my chair, to say nothing of leaping up and joining Reece on the other side of those tall chamber doors.

"What is your name, child?" he asks, stooping until his face is mere inches from mine.

"Nora Falcon, sir," I somehow manage to answer.

He smiles faintly, leans back.

"Nora," he says, trying it out for himself. "Nora, you can call me Lord . . . *Rothchild*."

I gasp.

"You, you mean . . ."

"Yes, child, that sorry excuse for a vampire is related to me."

"Your son?"

He snorts. "Heavens, no," he says with a weary shake of his head. "He is my nephew, and that, dear, is the only reason he is still breathing after his many, many mistakes. But you, my dear, have no such luxury."

I frown, sitting back in my chair.

And things were going so well between me and Lord Rothchild.

The Ancient eyes me hungrily, but no—it's just my chair. He signals to one of the Guardians behind me, who quickly slides Reece's vacant chair beneath the old vampire as if it had wheels and an I Break for Bathrooms bumper sticker on the back.

"That's better." He sighs, crossing his emaciated legs like a twig falling over another twig in the forest. "Now, dear, confess to Lord Rothchild your crime. Or should I say crimes?"

I shake my head and begin helplessly. "It was all a misunderstanding, sir. I mean, my lord. I mean . . . Lord *Rothchild*."

"Indeed." He sighs. "That is why you are here, Nora: to make us—to make me—understand. Now, do proceed."

"I didn't know I was breaking any laws when I killed a vampire or threatened to reveal the secret location of the conclave or alert the media or refuse to publish my book. I just—"

Lord Rothchild's eyes have grown cold and dark. "Ignorance is no excuse, my dear."

I nod, gaze cast humbly at my own lap.

He sits silently while behind him the six remaining Ancients murmur in agreement.

"These are very grave offenses, Nora," he says as they continue to murmur, or perhaps I'm just hearing more echoes tumbling around the high, vast room. "Any one of which would mean certain death, were your circumstances not so . . . peculiar."

"Peculiar?"

"Yes, dear. Despite my nephew's lack of impulse control, it appears he achieved one thing on this mission."

"Mission?"

"Do you make it a habit of parroting anything that's being said to you?" His fangs tremble as he surveys me with distaste.

"No, Lord Rothchild, no. I just . . . This is all so new to me. I wasn't aware I was the target of any mission."

"Dear," he says, patting my thigh with his clawlike hand, "impetuous as he may be, Reece would never have approached you were his mission not sanctioned by the Council of Ancients."

"You mean, then it was . . . *you* who sent Reece after me?"

"Of course, dear. Reece is many things, but a self-starter he is not. Like a child, he must be led by the hand. Who do you think was doing all the leading?"

I smile. "Then *you* were the one who read all my books?"

He laughs, a dry sound like paper crumpling under a heavy boot. "Of course, all four of them. I find them very entertaining, if not *entirely* accurate. We hope that in the future, you will attempt to correct some of those inaccuracies now that you know the truth."

"Of course," I answer too quickly.

He looks at me suspiciously. "Though it pains me to admit it, Nora, this Council *needs* you."

"But, my lord, anyone can write these books."

"Of course they can, dear, but it's not just the books we need. It's a keeper of the code. Now that you are one of us, now that you are immortal, we can hand off that particular duty to you. If you are willing, of course."

"Do I have a choice?"

"What do you think, dear?"

"I want to help," I insist, already knowing the answer.

"You want to *live*," he corrects.

I'm not sure what I am—who I am—constitutes as one of the living, but he has a point. "That too."

"Then so it shall be." He stands with the help of the much younger, but no less scary, Guardians behind him.

He leans precariously against the back of Reece's high, velvet-lined chair as he imposes my sentence. "Nora Falcon, kneel before the Ancients and accept your fate."

I do, the cold ground hard against my knees, and listen closely as Lord Rothchild decrees, "From this day forward, Nora, you are to be Keeper of the Code. No longer shall you write frivolous books for mortal teens, but instead you shall be our faithful chronicler, accurately describing the life of a young vampire for the thousands of teenage immortals just like yourself. The world of mortals is no longer yours. Your sentence is an eternity of servitude to us, the Council of Ancients, but also to your fellow vampires. Now rise and see about your friends. I have a feeling you will need their assistance in the centuries to come."

I stand, face Lord Rothchild, and bow graciously. It's not as easy as it looks.

By bowing I am accepting my fate, my future. My sentence.

I know the biggest part of me is simply accepting the inevitable, trading my willing obedience for survival, but the human part of me—that mortal soul that remains—knows that by pledging to keep, and use, the code for the vampires' purposes, I am dooming tens of thousands of mortals to their death.

Still, better to live today and hope to find a way to save all those mortal souls tomorrow, than to refuse and die without even trying.

Right?

A part of me is wistful as the Guardians lead me from the great hall, a walk that seems to take many long hours. Another part of me is hopeful that, in this new world, I can play a role to help humans and vampires finally understand each other.

Maybe it's naive to think so, but then . . . what else would I have to live for?

Before the great doors open with a grinding screech, I turn to look at the Ancients once more, but they have already left the room, their chairs as silent and empty as my future feels.

I turn toward the exit, a Guardian on each side, and face my sentence with a heart as heavy as the doors themselves.

# CHAPTER 32

The Healing Room is dark and quiet and staffed by vampires so old and neglected they might as well be zombies. With fangs.

And doctor's scrubs.

And more old-man slippers.

The Ancients must get a discount at Old Man Slippers "R" Us or something.

Abby lies lifeless on a marble slab, naked under a thin white sheet that extends from her clavicle to midway down her thighs. Her body is utterly motionless, her skin indistinguishable from the pale marble beneath it. She might as well be in a morgue, and in fact, it feels like she is. Despite all that's happened, my heart aches at the sight, the utter stillness of one who was once so vibrant.

We are not alone.

Her face is getting better as the thin, pallid vampires rub it constantly with a thick balm from silver urns positioned at strategic points alongside her body.

It smells not too strong or too weak: vaguely medicinal, musky, like the fat of dead animals, not humans.

"These are the Healers, Nora," Reece explains patiently, the right side of his face perfectly healed, the left side permanently scarred and as unsightly as any of the ancient vampires dotting this room. "This is their job; this is their specialty. If anyone can bring your friend back from the brink, they can. Though I warn you, it will be a long and arduous process for her. And, of course, for those who love and care about her."

I touch Abby's bare shoulder, and it feels lukewarm. Her eyes flutter open, no longer deep green but endlessly black and haunting, as if what they've seen has changed them irrevocably—has changed us all.

Still kind, though. She smiles, although it obviously hurts to do so.

One of her Healers starts to interrupt us, and Reece shoots him a look. The Healer acquiesces, bends back down to his work without so much as opening his dry, thin lips.

The room is filled with an eerie slick sound of thick, musky cream being worked into lukewarm skin, of slow and languid lathering.

I speak quietly, in honor of the stillness that fills the room. "Abby."

Abby croaks, "Nora."

"How are you, Abs?" I ask, eager to hide the shock I feel at the sound of her almost masculine voice. One thing Abby's always been is a girly-girl: heels and helpless giggles and French perfume and more eyeliner than she should wear during the daytime. To hear her sounding like a 360-pound wrestling announcer after a long night of smoking cigarettes and downing shots of whiskey has left me more shaken than I care to share with her. I wonder what her future, our future, will be like on the other side of mortality.

She shrugs and winces at the pain. Undeterred, she shrugs once more. "We'll see, Nora. The jury's still out on how normal I'll look once we get out of here."

"Just be glad we *are* getting out of here," I say, still shivering from my encounter with Lord Rothchild.

"Tell me about it. I've got reshoots all next week."

"Abby," I begin, tempted to lecture her about doing too much too soon.

"Nora, it's the best thing, for all of us. No matter how I look, no matter how cheesy they may be, the makeup crew on *Zombie Diaries* is the best. They'll get me in shape in no time."

"It *is* for the best," Reece says, and suddenly the mere sound of his voice fills me with an almost uncontrollable rage. "We can't have a world-famous actress like Abby going missing for too long. Whatever will the tabloids think?"

His distaste for what Abby does—for what I do—is obvious, but his words are reassuring nonetheless. There is a future, after all. We are getting out of this place . . . eventually.

What might happen then is anybody's guess, but if this experience has taught me anything, it's to be grateful for small favors—even when vampires are the ones handing them out!

Abby coughs up a load of phlegm that makes even Reece blanch, and suddenly the Healers shoot me dirty looks backed up by fangs and opaque eyes.

Reece puts a surprisingly gentle hand on my shoulder and tugs me away with a firmness that, despite our love-hate relationship, is impossible to resist.

Abby and I share a silent BFF wave with long, wriggling fingers as the Healers turn back to her with a vengeance, fingers dripping with lotion and goo, and I face the other new vampire in the room.

Wyatt sits in a modern black chair with a hole for his face, like those massage chairs they have in the middle of the mall that no one but pudgy businessmen ever really sit in, and only then to flirt with the pretty girls they always hire to massage their hairy (probably) backs. He's facing me and smiling mostly, wincing occasionally, as three female Healers (don't get all excited; they're twice as ugly as the guy Healers, which I didn't even think was possible) buff his back with circular loofah sponges slathered in thick white cream.

"Nora," he says, his voice sounding energetic. I soon see why.

His left arm is hooked up to an IV dripping fresh, thick blood.

Instinctively I lick my lips, protruding now thanks to my dangling fangs as the hunger tingles at the edge of my nervous system.

"How they hanging?" he grunts as a grody old Healer digs deeper into his back with the palm of her gnarled, clawed hand.

"Charming as ever," I say, walking to his side.

The Healers stop their scrubbing and pour a jug of clear water across his back to wash it dry. There are still scars, but I can see them fading, and they have come a long way from the open, exposed beef-jerky-strips look he was sporting when I shoved him into the backseat of Reece's Mercedes like a lifeless piece of bloody meat.

"Feeling OK?" I ask tentatively.

"Never better," he bluffs, tilting his head in Abby's direction. "How's she doing?"

I tsk, amazed that even as a vampire, I can still feel such strong jealousy. "A few hours ago you were ready to dissolve her in a holy water bath, Wyatt. Now you're worried about how she is?" The betrayal stings more than any harm Reece and his immortal fangs could do.

"That was then, Nora; this is now."

"It sure is," I grumble as Reece shuffles away to consult with Abby's Healers.

"So," Wyatt asks in a low voice as his Healers turn to add another helping of salve to their rough sponges before attacking his back once more, "what did the Ancients say?"

"I have to write vampire books," I confess glumly.

"That's *it*?" He lifts his face out of the hole in the massage chair to see if I'm pulling his leg. His eyes look alive and alert, his already thick lips looking even puffier—and ultimately more kissable—thanks to the fangs hidden deep beneath and the lifeblood coursing through his veins.

"Forever." I spit out the punch line.

"Oh," he says. "Well, consider yourself lucky."

"What do you mean?"

"The Ancients paid me a visit too," he confesses quietly. "Well, one of them anyway."

"Let me guess. Lord Rothchild?"

"One and the same." He smiles, though I can tell he's still in pain. "He said—get this—he said my punishment was to be your personal . . . *bodyguard*."

"Really?" I ask, a little too loudly, glad I can no longer blush. "What about Abby, though?"

"Let her get her own bodyguards," he jokes. "Better yet, let the studio get her bodyguards."

"Be serious," I say, slugging his shoulder and instantly regretting it when I see the look of pain cross his handsome face. "Sorry."

"Yeah, right. I dunno what Abby's punishment is. Lord Rothchild paid her a visit too and whispered something in her ear. She nodded and smiled, so it couldn't have been too bad.

But honest, I have no idea. Ouch!"

One of his Healers has pinched his back, signaling visiting hours are over.

We stand there in silence for a few moments, his head slowly retreating into the turtle shell of his ancient massage chair, me watching the Healers work wonders on his young, smooth back.

I hear quiet footsteps falling across the tile floor of the Healing Room behind me.

"Bye, Wyatt," I say as Reece tugs me away.

"Later," Wyatt says, wriggling his fingers at me before cooing to one of his Healers, "Faster, ladies, faster. I've got a swim shoot later this week, so don't let me down."

Outside the Healing Room the halls are quiet and, for the first time, quite empty.

I walk next to Reece for a while, assuming he's taking me somewhere.

Instead the halls turn into a maze of twists and turns.

I try to remember where we are, where we've been, to predict where we're going, but the walls Reece leads me past now are no longer sterile and white. Instead, they're varied colors, larger and then smaller, the floors wide and changing, and sooner than later I'm disoriented, at Reece's mercy to get me back to someplace safe.

When we are quite alone, without a Guardian in sight, he turns to me. "I know you think you've won." His breath is hot and redolent of fresh blood as it spills across my chest in waves.

"I don't, Reece. I—"

"You haven't." He takes a menacing step forward as I try, in vain, to hold my ground against his sudden ferociousness.

"Maybe you're safe for now. Maybe you're safe until the new book comes out, until your book signings are all over, until the interviews are all done and the eyes of the vampire world are off you for a little while, but no vampire—least of all *you*—is irreplaceable."

"But the Council." I know I sound pathetic but am powerless to control the quivering in my voice.

Reece's rage is a physical thing, causing his already distorted face to curl into a mask of pure and unadulterated hatred: hatred of just one thing—me!

"The Council," he spits back, "is outdated and impotent. My time is coming, Nora, and when it does, you and your friends back there are done for, finished, through. My power will be absolute, and there's nothing the Council—or you—will be able to do to stop me!"

His face is flushed, his fangs out, his claws eager and sharp, his head jutting forward as I back into a cold, stone surface that feels like exactly what it is—a prison wall.

"Fine," I manage to bluff. "Do your worst."

He laughs, an empty, broken sound that echoes through the gloomy chamber he's lured me into.

"Nora, my dear, I plan on it."

And with that promise, he turns and leaves me alone, his footsteps echoing down the long, winding corridor as his pace quickens and his rage slowly dissipates in the foul air he's managed to leave behind.

But I am not alone, for from the shadows appears an Ancient. But not just any Ancient.

"Lord *Rothchild*," I whisper, rushing to his side like a second grader who's just found his mom in the crowded mall.

"Nora," he says, not shying away from my vulnerable embrace.

I hug him, gently, because although he is obviously quite powerful, he is just as obviously quite frail.

"Follow me," he says after a time. He walks slowly but surely, as if his legs aren't as thin as broomsticks, as if his arms aren't trembling at his sides. Still, his body is firm, as if he's petrified, the organs long since withered and wasted away, and he's filled instead with solid granite.

The hallways seem brighter with his presence, and I realize that is because his Guardian walks behind us, a flickering torch in hand and a grim, unreadable expression on his face.

"Your young friends are almost ready for transport," he says as we turn down the endless tunnels through which Reece lured me so easily, so carelessly. "For obvious reasons, Reece will not be accompanying you on your return journey to Nightshade Academy."

"What will happen to him?" I ask, trying not to sound too concerned.

"To Reece? Nothing, I'm afraid. Laws are laws, and unless he breaks one more, we are powerless to stop him."

I follow him in silence, and he finally turns, just before entering the main entrance to the building.

"Don't fear, Nora. You will not be alone on your journey through this afterlife."

As if on cue, Wyatt and Abby are wheeled into the vast and glistening white foyer, smiling, though still pale and weak from their wounds. Abby is clearly the paler and weaker of the two.

"Safe travels," Lord Rothchild says before leaving me with them. "And remember, Nora, you are one of us now. Write like one of us."

# CHAPTER 33

The Creature crawls from the freshly dug grave, gray hands groping through the rich soil, pushing aside white maggots and earth to climb, one inch after the next, to the surface.

I stumble away from him, ridiculously high heels slowing my progress, getting stuck in the wet graveyard soil, tripping over broken, crooked headstones that snag at my black stockings and bruise my fair skin.

The Creature finally frees himself from the grave and begins his pursuit in earnest. His movements are slow but steady, his body a hulking shape of rotting flesh and gray bone, a face crammed with broken teeth and dark, empty eyeholes.

"Wyatt!" I cry, straining my voice, but I don't see him.

"Abby?" I yelp, limping backward as the Creature approaches and wrenching the small of my back against the top of yet another shattered headstone.

Abby too has abandoned me in my time of need.

Incredibly, I am alone again, running again.

Now the Creature stands to his full height of six feet or

so, grave dirt still tumbling from his moldy, blue burial tux. (Why are they *always* buried in blue tuxes?) Mildew and decay waft off him like smoke from a raging fire.

Still on my feet, for now, I back carefully away as the Creature finally regains his bearings. His skin is more green than gray, the moonlight glinting off his rusty cuff links and the silver fillings where his teeth used to be.

His hands are half flesh, half bone, the fingers skeletal. From the second knuckle back, gray rotting flesh resembles one of those half gloves the guys at school will wear to play racquetball or to ride their hybrid scooters to the nearest Smoothie Shoppe.

He looks around at first, spying the headstones, the skin around his missing nose sniffing for flesh, sniffing, sniffing, until at last he spots me and growls, his dead, dry vocal cords emitting a ragged screech that sounds like four hundred pieces of broken chalk scraping the same big chalkboard all at once.

I turn now and run, scampering as a thick gray mist floods the graveyard and threatens to obscure the hundreds of headstones scattered across my path.

I cough on the thick fumes, the Creature at my back, dead lungs not affected by the mist. I stumble blindly forward, the dense fog crawling up my ankles, thighs, hips, waist, and stomach.

Grass crunches behind me, earth moving in front of me as I stop to gag, my hands on my knees, my lungs on fire, my eyes watering, tears running down my face, skin itching, muscles burning like I've just run a marathon.

A hand on my shoulder makes me scream as—

"Cut!" yells a disembodied voice. I can't see because the

fog machine is going bonkers, causing my temporary blindness. Again.

"Harvey, what did I tell you about the mixture last time?" the voice is screaming, cutting through the fog and assaulting my ears as the tears continue to flow. "It's three parts water to one part fog juice, not the other way around. Didn't they teach you that at fog machine school? Let's regroup and start over. Nora, you all right?"

I laugh, taking the tissue Abby offers me as Wyatt pounds me on the back. "Yes, sir. Sorry. I just . . . couldn't . . . breathe!"

"Hey," says the director, a portly man in cargo shorts and a Hawaiian shirt, scratching his beard out of habit as he holds his ever-present bullhorn by his side. "You did the right thing. Better we burn through a few minutes of dead film than kill our guest star, right, Abby?"

"Sure, Norm." She pats his big belly familiarly, as if this is something that happens every night on set. "When you need us, big guy, you'll know where to find us."

With that Abby leads us off the graveyard set, past the half-empty and crumb-covered craft service table and the Porta-Johns to her camper, which isn't quite as big as I remember from my last visit to the set (was that *Zombie Diaries 2* or *3*?). It's still more than three times the size of our dorm suite back at Nightshade Academy.

"Budget cuts," Abby says by way of explanation as we crowd into the main sitting area. "The last one didn't do so well on DVD. They're hoping to leak this one online a few months early to generate more buzz. Until then, it's home sweet camper!"

I smile at her from my leatherback wing seat, looking for

any signs of scarring or disfigurement on her face and seeing none. Aside from a paler shade of skin, and the green contacts the makeup people have her wear "for continuity," she's the same old Abby.

"What, you drank all the Jolt Cola again?" Wyatt says, once again raiding Abby's dorm-size fridge as he bends down, giving us both a great shot of his derriere, which is irresistible even in his tattered fake-zombie costume. "I thought you had some kind of pull around here. You know I can't possibly drink this generic stuff."

"You'll drink it, and you'll like it." She tosses one of her promotional *Zombie Diaries* dolls—sorry, action figures—at his backside and misses. It lands in the sink with a clatter that echoes long after the doll's feet get stuck in the drain.

So much has happened since we left the Council of Ancients, all of it surprisingly good (you know, aside from the whole being immortal and having to drink blood for the rest of our lives part).

Wyatt has more work than ever. Abby, despite her grumblings, is lucky to be undead and more popular than ever, and Hemoglobin Press says the anticipation for the fifth Better off Bled book is off the charts.

I suppose I should be stoked, but it's pretty hard to get too excited when you know that buried within the pages, your book—*your* book—is a code only vampires can read, giving them directions to a place where after four days of vampire seminars and undead breakout sessions and dastardly meet and greets, they'll feed on the good people of Lake Hammer, Texas, like fat guys at an all-you-can-eat buffet.

I don't know how that's going to play itself out just yet, but despite Lord Rothchild's warnings, there is still a part of me more human than vampire. I keep waiting for it to wane, for myself to give in to the hunger, to become insatiable for blood, but so far I have been able to control myself fairly well.

Not that I'm any kind of saint, mind you, but I'm far from veering into Reece territory anytime soon, thank you very much.

Regardless of my own need to feed, the taking of another life—another *human* life—is something I've yet to experience and something I certainly don't want to accomplish because of my next book.

Still, I had to run the code as is, or Reece and the Ancients and every other vampire on this planet would know the jig was up and would come looking for me. (After all, my name is right there on the cover!) And not just me, but as Reece warned, everyone around me: Abby, Wyatt, fellow students, teachers . . . even our families and friends.

I was in it now, deep in it, for better or worse, and unlike one of my books, I couldn't just write my own ending and live happily ever after. This ending was going to be a lot stickier and then bloodier than even I could imagine.

But the conclave is still a few months away, and I still have time to plan before the good people of Hammer Lake are led to slaughter.

"Think fast!" Wyatt says, tossing me a fresh bag of blood from Abby's hidden supply.

"You sure you have enough, Abby?" I ask anxiously, desperate to slice off the silver foil seal and drain it dry before she can answer.

She shrugs. "It's cool. You guys go ahead. I've got a pretty good connection: a guy in the makeup department. He gets it by the case from the blood bank downtown every other day or so, tells them it's for research. He says the supply is pretty much unlimited, thanks to the hospitals being so particular about the blood supply lately."

"So, what?" asks Wyatt, those perfect lips centimeters away from his straw. "These are like . . . rejects?"

"Takes one to know one." She sighs without looking up from her latest script changes. "These in particular, I think he said, have, I dunno . . . hepatitis C?"

"Gross," he says, lips still hovering over the straw.

"Dude, I've been sucking them dry all week and look at me," she says, smiling healthily and looking none the worse for wear.

Wyatt and I shrug, sucking greedily until our bags are dry.

Without looking up from her precious script, Abby says, "You guys are gross."

A few seconds later, there is a knock at the door, and Abby's assistant swings it open to announce, "Abby, we need you on set."

Wyatt and I start to get up, but she smiles. "Not you guys yet. We just need to do a few reshoots, and then wardrobe will be back to get you, 'K?"

I smile as the college intern turns at the foot of the camper stairs and waits expectantly for Abby.

Abby gets up, sighs, and turns to us. "Before I go, I should warn you that the tech guys have this ray gun, see, like on *Star Wars*? It detects bodily fluids . . . so keep your hands to yourselves, or this is your first and last guest appearance in the latest installment of the Academy Award–winning Zombie Diaries franchise."

"Promise?" Wyatt asks before she slams the door. He sighs and takes Abby's seat, putting his feet on my chair and twirling it around.

When I swing back to face him, his lips are waiting for me.

# EPILOGUE

There is one at every book signing—the vannabes. Vampire wannabes.

The one approaching is tall and thin and strong, and if she didn't want to be a vampire so badly, she'd probably be really, really—I mean *really*—pretty.

Instead she covers her fresh, young face in pancake make-up, slathers her perfect, pouty lips in maroon lipstick, dyes her long hair a shade too dark, and covers her size-two body in outdated frills and drab collars in a size (or two) too big.

"Hi," I say, trying not to wrinkle my nose at the strong, spicy, no doubt dramatically named perfume she's wearing. "What's *your* name?"

"Countess Alexandra the Eighth," she says without a trace of irony, her steely young eyes daring me to dispute her.

I don't argue this time. I smother a sigh and just sign her new copy of my book, smiling but not too widely lest she see the faintest hint of the fangs lurking just below my upper jaw-line. They feel awkward and unsightly, although not a single person all night has commented on my appearance one way or another.

It's like when I had braces back in eighth grade. To me they felt big and awkward, and I could swear they were the first thing anybody saw when I approached, but no one ever noticed, and after a while I just started taking them for granted and basically ignored them.

I'm looking forward to the completely-ignoring-them phase, but I'm not quite there yet.

"Going to the conclave this year?" I ask Countess Alexandra the Eighth, signing my name with a flourish.

"Oh, uh, yeah, sh-sh-*sure*," she stammers, and not even three layers of pancake makeup can cover up the blush rising across her young, hollow cheeks.

"Supposed to be a *really* good time," I say knowingly, sliding the book back across my signing table.

"Yeah, can't wait," she continues to bluff, avoiding eye contact as she reaches eagerly for her hot-off-the-press, $22.95 copy of Better off Bled #5: *Scarlet's Sacrifice* by Nora Falcon. Yeah, yeah, I know what Reece wanted to call it, but . . . my book, my rules, my title. Besides, the title wasn't part of the message, anyway.

She tries to grab it off the predictably black tablecloth, but I hold it firmly until she looks at me, her face half-expectant, half-impatient.

"Hey, Countess," I tease, before finally letting the book go. "Be careful what you wish for."

She pauses, blinking twice, and in her confusion, I see the sad little seventeen-year-old hiding beneath the vampire costume.

Suddenly I am sad about taunting her, sad about pretending I'm any better than her simply for knowing something no human should ever know.

I feel vaguely bad that I am partly to blame for her ridiculous outfit, for her three layers of makeup, for her frilly name and the vials of fake blood she and the rest of her "coven" spread around freely every Saturday night as they light black candles and sip tomato juice and watch *Interview with the Vampire* for the four hundredth time, probably.

And I'm even sadder to think how many girls like her will be living and dying in Lake Hammer, Texas, this time next year. At least, according to every other vampire on the planet. For myself, I have finally cracked my own code: a way to help those poor humans in Texas and not alert Reece or the Council or anyone else before conclave. Another code, a human code, was included in my last-minute rewrite of the latest adventures of Scarlet Stain, and as soon as I reveal how to crack it, Hammer, Texas will be a ghost town long before the vampires show up. Of course, timing is everything, and it will take every ounce of patience I've had—plus a few acting lessons from Abby, of course—not to let Reece and the others know my dirty little secret. But it's out there, in every new copy of the book, in every bookstore, on every tablet, in every country, and eventually all will be revealed.

If I live that long, that is.

Countess Alexandra the Eighth smirks, clutching the book to her chest, and the moment is gone.

She disappears into the jostling, late-night bookstore crowd, joining her small "coven" of five identically clad friends as they slurp frozen mochaccinos through green straws and black-painted lips near the Books 'n Beans café.

I sigh, rub my eyes, and start to uncap a fresh Sharpie pen to sign my next book when a familiar face leans in and oozes, "Can you make mine out to Model of the Year, please?"

Wyatt smiles, his hair grown out, his chiseled features flawless, his pale hands outstretched eagerly.

Out of sheer habit, I grab the book. “You sure that won’t jinx anything?” I ask, signing it as per his request.

“You’re still my girl, right?” he asks, causing a scene in his tight, black jeans and white T-shirt, both looking as if they were designed just for him.

“I suppose,” I say coyly, adding a personal postscript.

“Then what do I have to lose?” He grins.

I shove the book back and smirk. “You always know just what to say, don’t you, player?”

He smiles, ignoring the impatient vannabes stamping their feet behind him as he opens the book to read my inscription.

I hazard a glance behind him, hoping for once that Abby has found time to show up.

He seems to know what, or whom, I’m looking for. “Reshoots,” he says, barely looking up from the title page of the book in his long, graceful hands. “She said she’d catch you next time.”

“Next time.” I violently snap the cap back onto my Sharpie even though I know full well I’m just going to have to use it in another couple of seconds. “Next what, Wyatt? Next book signing? Next decade? Next *century*? She hasn’t been to one of my signing in ages!”

He leans down, smiles, and whispers, “Hey, one out of two of us ain’t bad, right?”

I smirk and look up at him.

The weeks, then months, since Reece turned him have been almost supernaturally good to Wyatt. His skin, once tan, is now a marble, almost fashionable pale. The turning took what baby fat had made him so adorable before and evaporated it, leaving in its stead a lean, nearly fat-free Adonis. He was never a slouch to begin with, trust me, but now it seems his entire musculature has literally transformed into something else altogether. It's to the point now where I have to force myself not to gasp whenever he shows up like this, unannounced and unabashedly awesome. It seems almost cruel that a boy should look this good and yet still be mine.

His eyes are darker now too, his black hair shoulder length and flowing, his cheekbones even more pronounced. If anything, he's booked more jobs since becoming a vampire than ever before.

I'm happy for him but bummed for me. Now we spend even less time together, and I crave every moment he can steal away and simply be there by my side.

I watch his thin lips curl into a genuinely inspired smile as he reads his personal message from me:

*To my Model of the Year,*
*I look forward to getting between your covers later.*
*Your Girl*

He turns without a word, exiting the line.

With a collective sigh, the vannabes pause to watch him walk toward—appropriately enough—the romantic literature section.

Even his movements have changed, the way his muscles and bones join and flow together so that he doesn't so much strut as stride, like a panther stalking his prey.

I follow him with my eyes (me and every other girl in the joint) and see him turn and hug a girl.

I almost stand from my signing table to launch a twelve-pound, two-hundred-page hardcover book at her until I see a familiar face—

Abby!

She wears an expensive black tracksuit over her *Zombie Diaries* wardrobe and a ball cap to disguise her appearance, but I'd know that pert nose and familiar smile anywhere.

So she'd made it after all.

About damn time!

She gives me a guilty smile, which is pretty gratifying coming from a girl who hasn't genuinely apologized—ever, for anything—since we've met.

She too has blossomed since becoming one of the undead, her skin a surprisingly appealing slate of clean lines and sharp edges, her eyes once so lively now dark and alluring, her muscles more defined, her movements—like Wyatt's and like mine—more limber and self-assured.

She's even started doing her own stunts on the show and no longer complains when the shoot stretches overnight and she's able to give in to the insomnia all three of us have shared since the fateful events of that torturous, then freeing week that seems so long ago.

I smile, watch my best friends and fellow vamps stand next to each other, and reflect on where we've been, where we are, where we're headed.

Life hasn't been easy since I turned over those three flash drives to my editor at Hemoglobin Press, but it certainly hasn't been dull; that's for sure.

We still have our busy schedules: Wyatt with his constant modeling, Abby with her shoots and reshoots, me with the heavy edits my editor demanded—to say nothing of a full course load at Nightshade Academy.

And always, always, the danger from Reece is ever present.

Sure, he let us go after turning us, but then, what choice did he have?

The Council of Ancients decreed his punishment, and he was forced to abide by it, even if it meant his face would remain horribly disfigured for eternity.

And he certainly couldn't have turned in my book by himself, not without raising questions about why I wasn't doing it and where I went and what he did with me.

And so he let us go, swearing his oath of revenge that if we did anything to ruin the conclave, he would personally devour our worlds and torture us for the rest of eternity.

We believed him, but with the conclave less than a month away, that doesn't mean we still don't have a few tricks up our sleeves.

Now all we have to do is survive the first few days of the winter solstice.

If we can do that, our plan might just prevail.

Well, I'd hardly call it a plan—hunch is more like it, but it's better than nothing.

And after all, the lives of nearly thirty thousand people depend on us.

Hey, nothing like a little life-or-death pleasure to put oral reports and pop quizzes in perspective!

I hear a throat clearing, shattering me out of my reverie.

I look up and see another vannabe standing in front of me, book outstretched in pale, black-tipped fingers, toe tapping impatiently, dark lips curled into a permanent scowl that only manages to crease the heavy pancake makeup she has slathered on for my benefit.

"Name?" I ask, stifling a yawn and hoping she won't notice.

She doesn't. "Countess Cruella the Second," she says proudly, daring me to dispute her with dark eyes surrounded by even darker mascara.

I smile and sign per her request.

Around me, though I know the noise level hasn't changed any, the room grows silent and dark, as if someone has pulled a plug but only I can see the difference.

My cold skin tingles, and my nostrils flare involuntarily, but there is no smell to alert me, no change in the room's temperature to cause the sudden decrease in skin temp.

My hand begins to tremble around the pen between my fingers. My shoulders tingle as if someone is reading over my shoulder. I force myself to focus on my signature, slowing it down so my writing doesn't careen off the page and onto the tablecloth.

As I hand the book back, I suddenly realize the reason for my discomfort: a cloaked figure—dark, shadowy, and somehow vaguely familiar—lingers by the Books 'n Beans café. OK, so cloaks aren't *exactly* a rarity at these freaky late-night signings, but this cloak looks particularly authentic. Most of the costumes worn by my fans are amateurish at best, like curtains with the rods taken out or leftovers from Halloween rooted out of the clearance aisle in early November. The vannabes dress more authentically, but those are girls, and this cloak is definitely hiding a very male body.

I cut a glance to Wyatt and Abby, hoping they've seen, but Wyatt's showing off my autograph and Abby's making gag-me faces at it. Neither has seen, nor is likely to spot, the cloaked figure just beyond the line of fans and vannabes.

I strain my eyes, looking for something identifiable to

confirm this connection we seem to have, for some distinguishing mark or some reason I should be feeling the way I do, but there are too many people, too many distractions, to focus.

Countess Cruella the Second is blathering on about something book-related, something she obviously feels really inspired about, and I smile and nod, watching desperately as the cloaked figure fights against the crowd of fans to reach the bookstore exit.

I feel trapped and smothered and eager to get up and follow.

But I can't just stand up and desert my post, not with a line of a hundred or more fans still waiting for my autograph.

Besides, that would alert people, make them wonder why I'm acting so strangely, and as surely as I'd be following the cloaked figure, they'd be following me.

And where would I lead them? What if the man in the cloak is dangerous? Am I willing to lure innocent victims to their deaths just to satisfy my own morbid curiosity? No, there's still too much of the human in me to become that cruel that fast.

I do my best to ignore Countess, fan though she is, and watch the cloaked figure carefully. It's not easy. He's chosen his wardrobe well, black being the predominant color at a vampire book signing. But he is taller than most of the girls and more solid. Evil wafts off him, turning my stomach as if I suddenly opened a Dumpster full of decaying bodies.

I can't believe how revolted I am, how alert and reviled I feel simply at his mere presence.

Am I overreacting?

Or reacting appropriately to a threat?

To a very real, very present danger?

I'm still getting used to the vamp in me, still uncovering

hidden meanings and physical reactions I find hard to master with so much else going on in my life.

The shape pivots and sidesteps a random coven. He zigs, he zags through the boisterous, young, hormonal crowd, always careful to avoid showing his face.

I admit, I almost miss it myself. But then, just before he flees the store altogether and blends into the darkness outside, he can't resist glancing over his shoulder for one last look at the guest of honor.

I am waiting for him, purposefully, relentlessly . . . patiently.

I catch his glance. He turns away quickly, unsure of what to do, then stops, the door half open, letting in the chilly air of another October evening in Beverly Hills, and turns back.

Our eyes meet, or should I say, my eyes meet his eye. Singular.

The scar tissue looks even worse now, dead and decaying, like a gray stain across his permanently shut eyelid. I can't help but smile to see the damage I inflicted, little old me, with the very laptop he forced me to write *his* book on. If I thought he looked ugly before, it's only gotten worse. His skin is twisted and sallow, a cross between gray and yellow, the scars running like melted rivulets down his once-handsome face. It's like a mask, so rubbery and awful. Others must think it's fake. Only those who know better realize it's the real thing.

Somehow that makes it even worse.

The smile of satisfaction tugging at the corners of my lips infuriates him, and he exits roughly, nearly knocking down a trio of young Goths just showing up late for the signing.

They grumble but make way, the intensity of his scowl—to say nothing of the burnt side of his face—shocking the fake gaiety right out of them.

I watch him for as long as I can and then turn back to Cruella.

She is still talking, smiling, clueless to my anxiety and suffering, and I nod, hoping she can't see the goose bumps on my forearms or the hair on the back of my neck standing up or the bleak hopelessness splashed across my pale face.

She turns to exit the line, and I frown, unable to conceal my powerful emotions any longer.

Wyatt sees it, gives me a *What's up?* look from across the room as Abby, too, shows concern.

I think briefly of alerting them somehow to Reece's presence, but then I stop and remind myself: *It's not them he's after, is it, Nora*?

Instead I rub my eyes and put my clasped hands to the side of my head in the universal sign for *sleepy* and watch them smile with relief.

They turn to each other, whispering in their own intimate, before-we-knew-Nora secret language as I grab a fresh Sharpie to sign another hundred or so books before I can finally call it quits and collapse into bed for another few quick hours of sleep before the day begins anew.

As I greet another fan, sign another book, and begin the process all over again, I can't help but think how alone—how utterly and completely isolated—I am in this crowded room.

How alone I'll always be, singled out for destruction by an evil force more powerful than I can ever hope to be. How alone I'll always be until I can snuff Reece out for good and accept the fact that I will live forever.

As I look at the cover art while preparing to sign yet another copy of Better off Bled #5: *Scarlet's Sacrifice*, I suddenly realize the similarities between myself and my fictional heroine.

Now I too have a nemesis, though he is half as charming and twice as deadly as poor fictional Count Victus.

And, alas, I'm not alone in writing my own ending.

For Reece will surely play a part in whether I live or die—and how painful an experience each might be.

I open the book to the title page, look up, and smile at the next vannabe in line.

"Let me guess," I say, Sharpie poised for another autograph. "Countess Esmeralda the Fifth?"

"Close," says the pancake-faced teen. "Esmeralda the Sixth!"